Bought By the Billionaire

Billionaire Beginnings

A BDSM, Billionaire, Erotic Romance

Parts One to Eleven of the

'Bought by the Billionaire' Series

Written By Simone Leigh

Simone Leigh

Simone Leigh Publishing

An Imprint of Simone Leigh Ltd
20-22, Wenlock Road,
London,
N1 7GU

Contents

Part One

The Master's Maid

It's hot; stuffy and hot. I load my cleaning cloths and sprays onto the cart and push it along the corridor. It's a high-class hotel and normally it's very comfortable working here, but the air-con isn't working properly and so my daily job of room cleaning is very uncomfortable today. I take the elevator up to my next room, the penthouse suite and unlock the door. It is a stunning room, bright and sunny, and when I cleaned it through the day before, it smelled pleasantly of the occupant, a mixture of expensive aftershave and a musky male scent. The scent still lingers, in stark contrast to my own clammy and sweaty odor.

I consider the owner of the aftershave for a moment as I open the window to let sunshine and fresh air in. I saw him leaving a few minutes ago, so I know I am clear to clean the room. He was dressed *smart casual*, wearing an expensive jacket with a loose linen shirt; perfect in this heat; and tight black jeans cut to flatter his noticeably male physique. He strode down the corridor with a bouquet of beautiful red roses, a briefcase, and a gleam in his eyes. Despite the briefcase, he did not look like a man with work on his mind.

The room is clean and tidy, needing almost no work. In the office, I empty a wastebasket by the desk and dust the desktop. I make up the bed in the room I can access. Some of the rooms are locked. I am supposed to do everything - all the work, every time. Vacuum the carpet, clean the bathroom, dust all the surfaces, wipe the windows, but the room is so clean already that I think I can skimp.

I decide it is good enough and go to check the bathroom. Again, it is immaculate.

Why am I doing this?

I am hot, sticky, and tired, and working for minimum wage at a job I only took a few days ago to help me through my university studies. Already I hate the work, but I need the money.

The shower looks so inviting. Temptation wins. I kick off my shoes and quickly unbutton my tightly cut blouse. I immediately feel better as the cool air washes over my sweaty, glistening breasts. Unhooking my low-cut black bra, I drop it on my blouse and then unclip my hair. It is far too warm to wear my hair loose, but now freed, it cascades red and silky to my waist. Wriggling out of my short skirt takes only a moment, and my moist and sticky panties follow. I turn on the shower and step into the beautifully tiled enclosure.

The water feels wonderful on my skin and hair, coursing over my arms, breasts, and belly, taking the heat, sweat, and fatigue with it. I stand, stretching luxuriously in the warm stream, with the needles of water massaging me.

There is a click and the sound of a key in the lock.

I freeze. Here I am, stark naked, in the shower of one of the hotel guests. Has he brought his date back to the room?

Oh, God! What is his girlfriend going to say when she finds a naked woman in her boyfriend's shower?

Frantically, I turn off the water and reach for a towel, wrapping it around my naked torso to dry off as quickly as possible.

Oh, God! Oh, God. Oh, *God...*

Please don't let him come in here.

The bathroom door clicks open and the guy walks in. He has his back to me, but everything about him says *pissed off.* Has something gone wrong with his date? Still turned away from me, he almost rips off his jacket, hanging it up by the bathrobes. I can see him fiddling irritatedly with his tie as he slides it from around his collar and then hangs it with the jacket. He takes a couple of steps towards the mirror which has misted over from the warm shower.

He pauses, apparently noticing the steam and the misting for the first time and starts wiping the mirror with one hand. As the view clears, he sees me in the reflection, standing behind him, wrapped in a towel in his shower stall. He starts, then whips around, looking at first furious and perhaps alarmed, but then relaxing as he registers my complete harmlessness.

"I'm sorry. I was so hot. I'll go now..." I stammer.

"Oh, no need to be so fast," he says, grinning. "Finish your shower. Is there anything you would like to tell me?"

"Please don't tell anyone. I'll lose my job."

He smiles. "Is that right? Yes, I suppose it wouldn't look good, would it? Maid caught using guest facilities." He steps forward, still smiling. He really is very attractive, with deep blue eyes against tanned skin, and tall. "Are you going to make it worth my while not to tell anyone?"

One finger hooks itself around the top of my towel. He tilts his head to one side as he moves still closer, and his other hand takes a curl of my long, wet hair, twiddling it around a finger. “Beautiful hair you have there,” he says.

"I have to get back to work," I stammer. "I have other rooms to do."

"I'll tell the manager I had some extra cleaning for you to do - there's no hurry. I'm sure the hotel would expect you to... *service* the guests first..."

The finger tugs ever so gently at my towel. It parts and then slides down to the floor.

His eyes, meeting mine, smile as they follow the downwards path of the towel. I vaguely clutch at the damp cloth, but my heart isn't in it, and the towel continues its journey south.

"I think you owe me something," he says, and the towel finger wanders downwards between my breasts. I feel I ought to be frightened, but instead, my pulse is beginning to race.

He reaches back and pulls his tie from the hook. Quickly, he binds my wrists together, glancing briefly into my eyes as he does so, looking for a sort of permission. Then, pulling my arms up over my head, he attaches my bound wrists to the shower wall fitting. He stands back, cocking his head, admiring his handiwork. I stand there, naked as the day I was born, stretched up and tied for the perusal of a complete stranger. And yet, I am growing warm and wet.

His eyes lock onto mine. "And now, milady, let's see how well washed you are."

Placing one hand on my breast, he starts kneading as his mouth lowers to the other, first to suckle, and then nibble the nipple. His tongue circles, flicking the nipple to hardness. When he seems to feel he has a satisfactory result, his mouth and that tantalising tongue move to the other nipple, while his hand slides over my stomach, descending. I feel him outlining the curve of my waist, over my hip and belly. His fingers twine themselves in my curls before slipping in between my thighs.

I can hardly contain myself. Wriggling, I hear his chuckle of approval as he feels how wet I am. His tongue circles the nipple, one finger mirroring the movement over my clit. Torn between the desire to stay still and just let it happen, or to grind my hips around his hand, I find myself simply trembling helplessly and my thighs growing wetter and wetter, and warmer and warmer, and my pussy juice beginning to flow.

He pauses, standing upright. He looks into my face again, running his hands up and over and down my trembling torso, breasts, and shoulders, gauging my reactions. His pupils are wide and dark, and I know that he likes what he finds. Very slowly and gently, he runs his hands back around my shoulders and into my hair, pulling my face to his. He kisses me very softly on the lips and then starts nibbling at an ear.

"Enjoying this, aren't we..." he whispers. "Want to take things further?"

Do I want to? He's driving me wild. Tied up as I am, this stranger could do anything to me, but his slow, careful, caressing, and touching is arousing me far more than any *straight shag* could have. I am quivering with arousal, but I can't bring myself to reply. After all, he is still a stranger who has tied me up.

"Shy, eh?" he whispers again. "Let's see if we can fix that..."

With his head nestling into the curve of my neck and shoulder, he reaches behind me with one hand, firmly pulling my buttocks to him. I hear a clunk and then another, and I am puzzled.

"I thought I should play the gentleman," he says. "Time to take my shoes off." As it dawns on me, in my stupefied arousal, that he is still more or less fully clothed, his feet slide between mine, easing my legs apart. I stagger slightly, but his other arm takes my weight as I regain my balance.

"Now," he says. "Do I need to tie those ankles apart? Or do I get some cooperation?"

I still can't bring myself to speak. My trembling continues, and I am beginning to pant, my breath coming in short bursts and my colour rising. He knows exactly what he is doing to me.

"Still shy? We'd better sort it out then." He releases me slowly and stands up straight. "Don't move, Miss Silent," he says as he turns and walks out of the room.

For a minute or so I hear nothing, and then there is music, some kind of soft classical. It grows louder, and then he comes back into the bathroom carrying the roses I saw earlier and something else I can't make out. He has stripped off his shirt. His smoothly muscled torso bespeaks the kind of man who either has a very physical job or who works out, knowing that women don't go looking for overly muscled morons. In his bare feet and wearing just his black jeans, which are now bulging at the front; dark-haired, lambent eyed, and clearly with a purpose in mind, he is utterly, astonishingly, suggestive and inviting.

I could no more have said *No* than fly.

But I cannot quite bring myself to say *Yes* or, more appropriately; *Please.*

"I hope you like the music, Miss Silent," he says. "I think it's time we got some noise out of you. The music should cover it up in case anyone comes by." He brings the roses close to my face. "I did have other plans for this evening, but she stood me up. Would you like these? They are beautiful, aren't they? Do you like the scent?"

The scent is ravishing. What kind of woman stood this man up? I can't imagine. Delicately, slowly, he holds the roses for me to smell, and then, with only the very tips of the petals, he caresses my face with the flowers. The petals have small drops of water on them, and as he brushes my face and then moves down my neck, and over my breasts and stomach, the small cold droplets chill me and titillate at the same time. A moan escapes me, and I feel my pussy juices running below.

He smiles and raises his eyebrows. "Ahh... So you *can* make noises. Let's see what else you can do."

Abruptly, he turns away, and quite carefully, places the roses in the basin. He produces the *something* that I was unable to identify before - it is a spreader bar with leather ankle cuffs...

What kind of evening did he have planned before?

He looks at me and grins wickedly. "This might be even better than what I had planned," he says. He displays the bar to me. The cuffs look padded but strong. "She knew what to expect, but, well, I think you might be new to this... Hmmm? Still silent? Let's see what we can teach you."

I am panting uncontrollably now. He kneels and straps in first one ankle, and then the other. My feet are held firmly apart, my hands are tied securely above me, and my legs are spread wide.

He stands up and steps back, looking me up and down, just standing there, with his arms folded and his head tilted. Just looking.

"You are really beautiful, you know. With a figure like that, and your hair... What are you doing in a job like this?"

He comes close to me, almost but not quite, touching. I can smell him, warm and spicy, and I can feel his breath on me. I am longing for him inside me.

Carefully, and touching no other part of me, he reaches for and rubs my left nipple. The steam of my shower has cleared now and so I am cooling off. Under the influence of chill and arousal, my nipples are hard, crinkling with stimulation. He tweaks the nipple, smiles, and nods while *Hmmming* to himself.

He releases my nipple. Still touching no other part of me, he reaches down between my spread and dripping thighs. "You *do* like this, don't you?" Carefully - oh, so carefully - he touches my clit and delicately rubs it.

This time there is no escaping it, I moan uncontrollably and gush. My knees give way, but this time he does not support me, and my weight drops onto my tied wrists. I stagger upright, hobbled by my cuffed ankles. As soon as I am upright again, he repeats it, this time rubbing my clit a little harder.

I gasp and cry out as my knees buckle again.

"Good thing I put on that music," he says, as I pull myself upright again. "Don't want anyone outside hearing you yelp like that. But it's nice to know that you can make noise." He pulls quickly at my clit this time and then massages it for a moment. This time he holds me by the waist as my legs give way. "Don't want you hurting yourself in your enthusiasm," he whispers into my ear. "Tell me, what would you like to happen next?"

I am almost beyond reason. "I want... I want..." I can't get the words out. I can't bring myself to speak them.

His fingers make lazy circles around my clit and I gush again. I am frantic for something inside my pussy, but nothing is forthcoming.

"What do you want? You have to tell me." He now holds me very tightly, supporting my weight - my God, but he's strong. My legs are like string, but he takes my weight without effort.

"You have to tell me," he repeats. His fingers continue flicking and kneading my clit.

I am about to come, and I feel myself reaching the plateau. And he *stops.*

Still holding me by the waist, he takes his hand away. "You have to tell me what you want before it goes any further. I won't let you come until you tell me what you want me to do."

His hand slips between my thighs again and quickly, ever so briefly, his fingers stroke across my pussy; my lips are swollen, engorged, and sodden, and they pulse as one finger strokes between them and then withdraws.

I am almost frantic with lust. "Let me cum. Let me cum," I say.

"What do you want me to do?" His breath by my face is like a promise.

"I... I... I want..."

"You have to say it..." He kneads my clit quickly between two fingers, sending electric desire pulsing up through me. "You have to say it," he repeats. "You don't get it without saying it."

I surrender. "I want you inside me." If I wasn't tied and supported, I would collapse entirely. "I want you inside me."

He doesn't move. "That's better," he whispers into my ear. "You have to do better than that if you want to cum, but I can give you a little more now..." He slides a finger inside me, his thumb over my clit, and begins to work me. My climax, which had subsided a little, begins to build again immediately. He feels it. "Oh, no," he chuckles. "Oh, no, it doesn't work like that." His fingers withdraw. "What do you say?"

My mind blanks for a moment. Is he serious? What do I say? But my tormented clit and my aching pussy, brook no argument. "Please," I mumble.

"That's better." His finger brushes over my pussy lips. "But, 'please' what?"

I gasp and moan, writhing in my restraints and his grasp. "Please make me cum. Please fuck me. Please. Please fuck me."

"Now we've got there."

He kisses me full on the mouth, making sure I am standing up, and then pushes two fingers up inside me, hard. I feel them almost scrape against me inside, against my G-spot. I cry out, but he has already withdrawn and is down on his knees, his face to my thighs. From my rather awkward position, I look down to see him looking back up at me, at my face. As he looks, his hands are working, parting my curls to reach my pussy lips. He leans forward, and for one delicious moment, I feel his tongue swirl around my clit.

This time, there is nothing half-hearted or restrained about my reaction. I scream, just in time to feel him pull my thighs fully apart, and his tongue lick up from the back of my cunt, through and over my pussy lips.

And he stops.

I hang, my weight on my wrists, making incoherent gasps and wishing there was something I could say.

He pulls away and stands, smiling at me, as I am standing there in my shackles and my own sweat and juices. "This won't do you know," he says. And he turns and walks out again.

I can't believe it. I finally put together a sentence. "You can't do this to me! You can't leave me like this!"

His voice drifts through from the lounge. "Well, you didn't think I'm going to tongue-fuck you in that condition, did you?"

What?

What?

The sound level of the music goes up. And up again. And I wait.

He comes back in, again carrying something, which he puts on a shelf. I strain to see what it is - a toiletries bag? And he immediately leaves again.

A moment later, he is back, and he puts something else in his pocket.

"I turned the music up again," he says. "I think that when I get you properly Mastered, you're going to be quite the little screamer. We'll keep it private, shall we?"

That grin again. He stands for a moment, seeming to be savouring the situation. Then, stepping forward again, he says, "Just to keep you on the boil," as he holds me around the waist again, while pushing one, two, and then four fingers up inside me. Again, I writhe and pulse, on the brink of orgasm, as he finger-fucks me once, twice, thrice, and then stops.

Padding over in his bare feet to the shelf, he pops something in his pocket and then opens the *toiletries bag* - it *is* a toiletries bag - and takes out a razor and a can of shaving cream. "I like the taste of pussy," he says, "But not a mouthful of seaweed." He kneels in front of me again and aims the can over my crotch.

I recoil, trying to back into the shower stall. "No!" I say. "No, you can't do that."

"Really? No?" He pauses. "If you say no to this, then it's no to everything." He parts my pussy lips and takes a lingering lick over my clit, flicking me with the tip of his tongue. My resolution crumbles.

"Well..."

"Perhaps I can help with your decision." He reaches into his pocket and pulls out the *something*, and I hear a low buzz, and then a high buzz.

"Just something to keep you occupied," he says and pushes the egg up inside me. He does it slowly, sliding it along my engorged lips and up past my aching pussy muscles so that I feel every inch of movement.

Then, with the egg buzzing inside me, he sprays the foam and sets to shaving away my curls. He takes his time, is careful and thorough. A few minutes later, my crotch is as naked as the rest of me. "I don't like the taste of soap," he says, "and you are getting a bit sweaty." He reaches for the showerhead, turning it on full, but cool. He aims the fine needles of water over my breasts, concentrating on my nipples. I squirm and squeal. The water is just cool enough to make me react without chilling me.

"S'cuse me," he says, reaching up inside me with a couple of fingers, and popping out the egg, which is still buzzing. He negligently tosses it onto a towel, and then, turning the showerhead upside down, he sprays squarely up into me, over my pussy and my clit with the water. Water, lather, and heated juices run down my legs as I struggle and squeal against the intensity of it all.

The sheer scale of the stimulation is beyond bearing. I scream, trying to escape the intense pleasure, pain, and overstimulation of the needle jets. I am about to climax uncontrollably.

And he stops - again.

By now, I am almost delirious with the desire to cum, and I sag in my bonds, head bowed.

"You said that you still have some work to do?" he asks. "More rooms to clean?"

"What?" I raise my head to look at him. Is he really suggesting...?

"You *do* have work to do. We don't want you getting into trouble with your boss, do we? I've met Mr Chambers and he's not really a very nice man."

He reaches above me and starts undoing the tie. "I think you should go and do your work, and then I can finish you off later." The tie comes loose, and he starts dressing me, slipping my arms through my bra straps, and hooking me up at the back.

I stare unbelievingly. "You can't be serious? After all that, you want to just break off and I'm supposed to..."

He interrupts me. "Get dressed and come back later. That way you won't lose your job, and I'll know that you really do want me to fuck you..." He smiles as he buttons up my blouse. "Now, here's your skirt. Pop that on... and no, you don't need those." He takes my panties away from me, tossing them into a corner. "Lift your feet, one at a time."

I step into my skirt unresistingly as he pulls it up and zips me up. "And before you go..." He retrieves the egg and slips it, buzzing quietly, up inside me. "I'll expect to find that still there when you come back. You just practice gripping it so it doesn't slip out - that would just be embarrassing, wouldn't it?" He roughly towels my hair dry and gives me a brush.

He pushes me out and towards the door. As he propels me into the corridor, brush in hand and buzzer within, he whispers, "What's your name?"

"Elizabeth."

"I'll see you later, Elizabeth," he says.

The Story Continues in 'The Master's Contract'

Part Two

The Master's Contract

I stand in the corridor, speechless, but gasping.

A complete stranger has brought me to the verge of the most explosive orgasm ever and then stopped, shoving me out into this corridor to carry on cleaning hotel rooms.

What the fuck am I supposed to do now?

I stare at the closed door and want to shout the question at its blank surface, but if I was heard shouting in the hotel, I might lose my job. I could cry over the sheer let down of what has just happened.

Reaching into my pocket, I pull out a hair tie, pinning my long red locks, still damp from the shower, back onto my head. I start to step towards my trolley, full of cloths and brushes and furniture polish, but as I move, I am brought to a sudden stop by the vibration of the egg, still whirring away inside me. I yelp and then clap a hand over my mouth in case anyone hears me.

The door opens again. *He* stands there, wearing an arrogant smile. "Still here, Elizabeth? I said to come back later. What time do you come off-shift?"

"Er, seven o'clock."

He nods. "Fine. I'll see you at five past seven. Don't be late. I'll be waiting for you." And he closes the door again.

I can't believe the gall of the man. Does he think I am going to come running, just because he asks and appears to expect it?

Then I admit the truth to myself. Yes, of course, I am going to come back. The man, whoever he is, is devastatingly handsome and has just played a game that brought me to the edge of a crashing climax.

Correction: is *still* playing a game.

I check my watch: five-thirty, an hour and a half still to go. Might as well get on with my work.

Walking awkwardly because of the egg buzzing away inside me, I push the trolley along to the lift. There are no other rooms on this floor. The penthouse suite stands alone. I wonder who he is, to be able to afford to stay here.

For the next hour and a half, I work in a bit of a daze. Fortunately, I have no real problems with any of the work, because were I to have to bend over, for example, the whole world would see that I'm not wearing any panties. *He* has those, discarded on his bathroom floor. The egg works sporadically, sometimes resting quiescent inside me, but then bringing me upright with a gasp as it suddenly vibrates to life. My pussy juices are running, working their way down my thighs.

Seven o'clock comes and I put my trolley back in the utility closet. I am wondering what excuse I can use for going back up to the penthouse, but as I pass reception, Ricardo calls me from the desk. "Hey, Beth. Penthouse wants a bottle of champagne. Can you take it up to him, please?"

Ricardo shouldn't have asked me to do it. There are other staff for room service, but I am not about to complain. The timing is perfect. I collect the champagne on ice, trying not to bend over as I push the bar cart along, and take the lift back to the top floor.

Suddenly nervous, I hesitate before tapping on the door, but almost before my knuckles touch the wood, the door opens, and he is there again. I glance up. Of course, there is a camera by the lift, he knows exactly who is outside his door.

He smiles a welcome. "Ah, Elizabeth, lovely to see you again. Do come in." He takes the champagne cart from me, and I follow him inside. "I hope you don't mind or think me forward," he says, "But I've made a few preparations for you."

Preparations?

I halt and then jerk as the egg buzzes inside me again. An hour and a half of it working inside me has left me almost limp with desire, and desperate for a real fuck.

He looks pleased with my reaction. "Ah, you *do* still have it inside you. Nice to know that you can follow instructions." He holds up a small box and jabs a button on it as I watch. The egg inside me jolts to life again, sending electric arousal up my spine. I yelp. "Good girl," he says. "That's what I like to see. *Obedience.*"

Suddenly, he steps up close, circles an arm around my waist and brings his mouth to my ear. "Don't need the help now, though, do we? I just wanted to keep you on the simmer until your return."

His free hand strokes my cheek, slides down over a breast, cupping and squeezing briefly, and then continues its way down to the hem of my too-short skirt and under. I am unbelievably aroused. Beginning to pant again, I can only ask myself how a stranger can be doing this to me, as his fingers journey up and in, stroke past my clit and up into my swollen pussy. He flicks out the egg and tosses it onto a side table.

"Go have a shower again, Elizabeth," he says. "You're hot and uncomfortable from working. I want you relaxed."

Even in my inflamed condition, I must admit that this is a good idea. I nod and walk to the bathroom.

Stepping into the room, which is still steamy from my earlier visit, I start to unbutton my blouse, but I can't be bothered and simply lift it up over my head. For a moment, my vision is blocked as the blouse goes over my face, then, as I can see again, I realise that he is in the room with me. I startle, and he grins. "Don't mind if I watch, do you?"

I shake my head dumbly.

He nods in satisfaction. "I might decide to help, but let's see how it goes." His grin drops to a half-smile and he tilts his head in that expression of his that I am coming to recognise. "Take your bra off, Elizabeth. Slowly. And turn to face me. I want to see you properly."

Turning to face him fully, I unclip my black and lacy bra, then slide it slowly down my stomach, before letting it drop to the floor. Then I start to unzip my skirt.

"No," he says. "Not yet. Fondle your breasts, Elizabeth. Caress them. Play with your nipples."

He wants me to perform for him?

I hesitate.

"I'm waiting."

I cup my own breasts, then, stroking and squeezing them, I watch his gaze drop to watch. Suddenly, I realise that I very much want to give him a show. I start tweaking and pinching at my nipples, making them crinkle and harden. I feel myself warming from within and flushing. He smiles again, knowing exactly what is happening. He really does have the most beautiful smile, starting at his lips and curving up to his deep blue eyes.

"Don't move. Stay right there," he demands as he walks out, returning only a moment later with the champagne bottle. "We'll drink this in a while, but I have better uses for it right now."

The bottle is chilled from the ice, running with condensation. He holds the cold glass up to my nipples, flicking over their already crinkled skin with the icy surface. I gasp at the sheer combination of pleasure and pain of the sensation, not cold, just stimulating. "I'm going to enjoy training you, Elizabeth," he says.

"Sorry? Training me?"

"You'll see," he says. "I'm going to fuck you raw in a while, but first you have to please me. You have to be a good girl."

I groan. Desperate to fuck, I want nothing more than to feel him inside me. "Oh, God..."

"Yes, Elizabeth? What is it?"

"Please..."

"Please, what?"

"Please. I... I need to cum."

"So, what would you like me to do?"

"Please..."

"I told you before, you have to ask. You won't get it without asking."

I am almost incoherent with lust. "Oh, God. Fuck me. Please, fuck me."

"Good girl. That's better."

Abruptly, he pulls me close, kissing me hard on the mouth, lingering as he runs his fingers through my hair. Twisting me around, he bends me face down over the hand basin. From somewhere, he produces a silk cord, obviously having it already prepared. He loops it over my left wrist, around a tap, then around my right wrist and the other tap. I am tied down, with my back arched, and my butt presented to him.

With my face down, I feel him come close behind me and pull me by my waist backwards, until my arms are outstretched and my hips pulled upright. His pelvis is pressed against me and I can feel his erection. Pushing my skirt up around my waist so that my naked derriere is exposed, with one foot, he spreads my legs, stretching my aching pussy open.

He splays himself over me. I had realised he's tall. I am not short, about five feet nine, but to bend over me like that, he must be well over six feet. His voice murmurs close to my ear. "Now then, Elizabeth. You've been good and asked nicely, so you deserve something. Which do you want? My cock inside you? Or do I tongue fuck you?"

Shaking and trembling, I can barely speak, and gasp out, "Don't care. Just let me cum."

"As my Lady wishes." He backs away from me, and the next thing I feel is his tongue, not gentle this time, but licking hard and slow from the front, over my clit, and beyond, before making circles inside and around my pussy. I cannot help myself, and I come within seconds, breaking into helpless screams as pulses of pleasure pump through me. I try to buck, but he grips me firmly around the pelvis and continues his merciless probing.

When I can bear no more, when I think I am going to explode, I shriek, "Enough. Enough!"

He stops instantly and as I hang slack and limp over the basin, panting, he strokes one hip, and I feel him kiss my bud.

He stands up, untying me. For a moment, I don't move; I don't feel capable of moving, thinking my knees will buckle if I try. As my breathing subsides, he lifts me upright, taking my weight for a moment, holding me to his chest. "Are you all right, Elizabeth?"

Speechlessly, I nod, then, as I become able to support myself, he says, "Have your shower. I'll see you in the lounge. Don't bother with the skirt."

The shower is blissful, and I alternate with hot and cold jets, spraying the water over my breasts and stomach. My pulse is slowing and my breathing is returning to normal. The shampoo and the soap are wonderful, expensively perfumed, and I inhale deeply through the steam.

Stepping out, the towels are huge and fluffy. Only the best in this suite.

Although I have been told to leave my skirt, I do not quite like to step naked into the room. I shake my head. *Shy?* I have just allowed a man I only met for the first time two hours ago, to tongue-fuck me to orgasm, and now I'm bashful about it?

I dry my hair so that it falls long and loose around my tiny waist, and then step into the lounge wearing a white bathrobe.

He looks up from where he is pouring champagne into two glasses. "Ah, there you are. I thought I might have to come looking for you."

I suddenly feel awkward again. "My hair takes a long time to dry."

Now, looking at me admiringly, he comes up close, lifting my long tresses, holding them to his face, and breathing deeply. "Yes, and beautiful hair it is, Elizabeth. By the way, time for a formal introduction. I'm Richard."

He holds out his hand and, a little confused, I take it. "Nice to meet you, Richard."

"Sit down." He gestures to one of the expansive settees, positioned to take in the spectacular view over the city. He passes me a glass. "Sit down," he repeats. "Let's talk a little before we move on to other things."

It is good to know that talking is an option, but... "Other things?" I ask uncertainly.

He smiles that tilt-headed smile of his again. "You didn't imagine we'd finished, did you? No, not by a long way. The evening is young."

I hide my confusion in the glass, sipping at the drink.

Richard refills it and sits beside me. "Don't worry. I'm not going to get you drunk. We've already established that I don't need to, haven't we?" He looks me full in the eyes and then continues. "Tell me, Elizabeth. Why are you cleaning hotel rooms?"

Why is he asking me?

I shrug. "I need the money. I've got to get through college and my parents can't help much."

He nods. "I thought it might be something like that. Do you enjoy the work?"

I think it is a silly question. "No, of course not. It's lousy work, but it's work."

"What are you studying at college?"

"Business studies."

"Not just a pretty face, then, or a beautiful body." He nods, raising his eyebrows, seeming to be thinking about something. Then he stands, holding out a hand to me. "Come along, Elizabeth. Time to move on."

When I hesitate, he wriggles his fingers at me, his eyes pointing to a door.

The bedroom?

I take his hand, and he helps me from my seat. He is amazingly sexy. His smooth, tanned skin highlights his dark, but slightly greying hair and deep, deep blue eyes. As I rise, he fixes me with those eyes. I could lose myself in those eyes.

He takes my other hand also, and facing me, he leans forward, kissing me on the mouth, soft and full. I lean into the kiss, hungry for more, hungry for whatever he is offering.

He leads me to the door and opening it, stands to one side, letting me in first.

It is a bedroom, but I wonder how much sleep it sees. A huge room with an entire wall of glass, it overlooks the city far below. A large bed, made up with white silk sheets and pillows, is scattered with rose petals. For a moment, I think the petals are also silk, but then a heady perfume tells me they are real. The corners of the bed are posted in black wrought iron and from each post dangles a chain ending in a cuff.

The lighting is low, flickering in the glow of candles, and with a real fire in the hearth. My eyes slide past wardrobes and drawers, a thick fur rug spread out before the fire. I can only look at that bed. This is a room of fantasies, of dreams.

"Do you trust me, Elizabeth?"

Do I trust him? I have only just *met* him. But then, I have already allowed him to tie me up, twice. He could have done anything to me, helpless as I was. "Yes, I trust you."

I hear the smile in his reply. "Good, because I want to be your Master, and for that, you must trust me."

As I try to digest what this means, he pushes me forward to the bed. I think he wants me to get onto the bed, but he stops me, and turning me to face him, he starts to untie the belt of the robe I am wearing.

"I'm not - "

He stops me speaking, putting a finger to my lips.

"Shhh..." he says, very quietly, looking me in the eyes. "I am your Master now, and I have not given you permission to speak. Do you understand?"

I nod my head.

"Good. For now, the only things you may say are either to ask for more or to ask me to stop. But if you *do* ask me to stop, *everything* stops, and you will be going home. I will tell you what to do, and you will obey, or you will go home. Do you understand?"

I nod again, and he smiles in satisfaction. "Good. Now, take off the robe, Elizabeth. I want to look at you."

I shrug the robe from my shoulders, standing naked for him. He looks me over very carefully, his gaze examining me - my breasts, my waist, my sex. He starts to circle me. Involuntarily, I start to turn to follow him.

"Did I tell you to move?"

I shake my head and stand still again. Now, I feel his hands on my shoulders, from behind, his fingers sliding over my arms, my stomach, my buttocks, and my thighs. Despite my amazing orgasm only a little while ago, I am feeling warm inside again.

"Get on the bed, Elizabeth. Lie on your back."

Obediently, I climb onto the silken sheets, rose petals scattering under me.

"You're so beautiful, Elizabeth. I love beautiful things. Do you like the bed? Is it not beautiful too?"

I nodded silently.

"Open your legs, Elizabeth. And raise your knees. Show me yourself."

I hesitate.

"Do you want to go home?"

I shake my head.

"Then do as you are told. I want to see all of you. Show me your pussy."

A stab of desire runs through me, and as I open my pink folds to him, I'm growing wet again.

He sits on the edge of the bed, examining me, one finger running over my stomach as he looks. "Touch yourself, Elizabeth. You're not wet enough yet. I want to see that you are ready for me."

I slide my hands down to my clit, rubbing and tweaking, lust rising in me rapidly. He watches for a minute or two, then rises and goes to a cupboard, his eyes never leaving where I am playing with my sex. Pulling something from the cupboard, he tosses it to me, then he pulls a pillow from the bed, and with little effort, lifts my hips from the bed, slipping the pillow under me.

"Now use that," he commands. The gentleness is leaving his voice now, but I am becoming too excited to care.

Taking the vibe he has given me, I start working myself with it. Distracted for a moment by the sensations running through me, I close my eyes, my pussy getting hotter and wetter, and my pussy juices running down my thighs onto the beautiful sheets. The feeling of giving my all to this beautiful stranger rides me ever higher.

Opening my eyes again, I see Richard is taking off his shirt, watching me all the time. As he starts undoing his belt, he says, "Not just your clit. Inside you. I want to see you fuck yourself."

The vibe glides into me easily, my slit is slippery and hot, and the small, attached finger vibe is working my clit too. My orgasm is starting to rise again.

Richard sees it too and snatches the vibe away from me. "Enough," he says. "No one gave you permission to cum."

I lie there, dumbly looking at him, wondering what is coming next. His jeans are bulging, and as he removes them, I see his massive erection, firm and stiff against his navel. Can I take that much?

He sees where I am looking and guesses my thoughts. "Yes, you're getting it. All of it, *if* you are good and do as you are told. Off the bed, Elizabeth. Stand in front of me."

Compliantly, I obey, and not sure where to look, cast my eyes down. He leans to one side, and opening a drawer, takes out a single red silk scarf, then others. Using one of them, he blindfolds me, binding it tight around my eyes, then he leads me a few steps by the hand.

"Bend forward."

Again, I obey, and feel first my left wrist, and then my right, being bound to something. The bedposts?

As earlier, he lifts me from the waist, positioning me with my hips up and my pussy exposed. My legs are spread, and my ankles are bound also. I am utterly helpless and completely exposed; I am at the mercy of this man. My pussy lips are swollen and aching, and my juices are running down my thighs. I have never felt so utterly aroused, so utterly ready for whatever would happen next.

Quivering and trembling, I hear him speak again. "Just to remind you, Elizabeth, you can tell me to stop at any time, but if you do, everything stops, and you go home. Say yes if you understand."

"Yes."

I am almost palpitating now to have my Master inside me. His penis pushes against my pussy lips and I move my hips to accommodate his huge erection, tilting myself for easy access. The vibe was a poor substitute for what I really want. I pulse with arousal, frantic now to have that cock, to swallow it within, to take it as far as it will go, balls-deep into me. Once, twice, it pushes against me, easing me open, slippery and wet. My pussy muscles jump in reflex, tightening around my Master, as he hesitates on the brink, not yet penetrating, not yet filling me as I want.

"What do you want, Elizabeth? You may speak."

I don't hesitate. "Fuck me. Please, fuck me."

His penis eases against my pussy and my muscles twitch. I lean back as far as I can, to take it, but again, he pulls away.

"That's not good enough, Elizabeth."

"Oh, God, please fuck me."

"Not good enough, Elizabeth. I have to really know what you want. You won't get it if you don't tell me."

I scream. "Please. Please fuck me with your cock! Bury yourself in me. I want to be fucked."

"That's better."

He thrusts hard inside me. My pussy walls take him easily, I am so wet and swollen, but he is huge, and I feel him bang against my inner wall, then again, harder. It hurts, but I am beyond pain or pleasure and know only that I want more of this. I feel my Master grasping my buttocks, holding me still as he fucks me. Repeatedly, his shaft spears me. I cry out in rhythm with his thrusting, again and again as he plunges deep inside me. I cannot move. I cannot see. Blind and spread-eagled, all I can do is scream in response to the pain and pleasure of my Master fucking me.

Climax wells up from within, mounting and building, threatening to take me completely. Then in a shattering crescendo, with my heart pounding and pulse racing, orgasm overwhelms me, and my cries turn to screams with my body's release. Still, he pounds inside me, plunging and thrusting, but I feel him now, leaning over me, arms wrapped around me, kneading my breasts, his breath ragged next to my face. He spasms as he bucks and presses into me, pumping his load. His hips jerk convulsively once or twice more, and then he relaxes and sighs.

"Good girl, Elizabeth," he says quietly. "Yes, that was good."

Withdrawing, he unties me, steadying me as I stand a little uncertainly, and he then removes the blindfold. My breathing is still quick, and he is flushed and panting, his hair sweaty and disordered. He smiles as he catches my eye, tossing me the bathrobe. "Shall we finish that champagne now?" he suggests.

I nod, uncertain as to whether I am permitted to speak, and he takes me by the hand, leading me back into the lounge.

On the fur rug, we sit in front of the fire, me cross-legged in the bathrobe and he naked in the firelight, his deep blue eyes lambent in the flames.

"I want you to come here again tomorrow, Elizabeth."

Again? I am not sure I can cope with another night like this so soon. But my body betrays me. At the suggestion that I could have such magnificent, stupendous sex again, that my Master might again take me to the brink and beyond, my heat starts to rise again inside. Bewildered by the scale of my own lust, I gulp at the champagne. Bubbles shoot up my nose, making me sneeze.

He laughs. "Is that a yes?"

I waver. "I'd like to, but if the manager knows that I've... well, you know... with one of the guests, I don't know what he'd do."

He stays silent, pursing his lips slightly.

I continue. "I'm sorry, but I really need this job. And, no offence, you're great, but you're a guest. You'll be moving on in a few days, and I'll be left high and dry."

He steeples his fingers, holding them up to his lips. "Elizabeth, I understand you, but you don't understand me. I will not be moving on. I live here. And you will not lose your job, because I will make sure you don't."

I'm confused. He lives *here?*

"Elizabeth, I live here in this suite. I own it. I own the hotel, in fact, along with quite a lot else. I have other houses, out in the country, but I live here most of the time because my business is here. Over there, actually, in that office building there." He points out of the window across the city to the Towerpoint offices. "And for the avoidance of doubt, I own those too."

I goggle. I've just been shagging with *Richard Haswell.* "Oh!" I say.

He laughs. "That impressive, eh? Listen, Elizabeth. Here's the deal, if you want it. You don't have to take it. If you say no, then I'll say nothing to anyone, and you can go back to cleaning rooms for a living."

Running fingers through his hair, he is clearly choosing his words carefully. "You come here, whenever I ask you. I will wine you, dine you, and buy you beautiful things. You will want for nothing, but you will do my bidding. I am your Master, and you will do anything I ask of you." He pauses. "I don't think you will find it unpleasant. I think you enjoyed yourself as much as I did this evening."

I gulp as conflicting thoughts race through my head. "Um, yes, thanks. It's a great offer. But why me? You must have a hundred women chasing you. What about my college? I wasn't looking for a life as a kept woman. What happens when you get bored with me? And I've thrown my college education away?"

"Fair point, and fair questions," he says, sitting close again, looking into my face. "Yes, you're right. I can take my pick, but there are always strings. I have a casual date with some money-seeking huntress and suddenly find that I'm supposed to have offered marriage, a house, and fifty thousand a month for housekeeping. Somehow, I've taken advantage of her and ruined her reputation. Next thing I know, I'm up to my ears in lawsuits. This is a *no-strings* offer, Elizabeth. If you accept it, we'll have a contract. I am not your boyfriend. I am your Master, and in return, you will have everything you want. Your college? You don't have to give it up. Quite the opposite, you should pursue it."

He bites his lip, thinking. "How's this then? I will pay your way through college - fees, living expenses, the lot. And you'll have a credit card to get anything else you need. You're doing business studies, you said?"

I nod.

"I assume they like you to get some practical experience with a big corporation, as well as the academic material?"

I nod again.

"Right, then you'll get that experience here in my company, in that office over there." He points again at the office block. "You serve as an intern there and get your business experience that way." He holds out his hands to me as I listen, dumbstruck. "Actually, it's perfect. You can take your pay through the internship. That covers you against any... embarrassment... as to where your funds are coming from." He looks me in the eyes. "What do you think?"

Those blue, blue eyes stare into mine. At some level, I feel that I should be outraged. This man, who I only met earlier today, is offering me a position as his personal... what? Concubine? Mistress? Whore? Call girl?

But it doesn't feel like that. I *like* him. And he seems to like me. And if I could concentrate on my studies instead of cleaning up rooms after some jerk has had too much booze and thrown up...

He is still silent, gazing steadily into my face.

I make up my mind. "When do I start?"

He nods and smiles, then looks at me and says, "When do I start, *Master?*"

Yes, of course. I cast my eyes down. "When do I start, *Master?*"

"Right now," he says cheerfully, but then pauses. "Outside this apartment, a simple *Sir* will be sufficient I think."

"Yes, Master. And what would you like me to do, Master? Right now?"

"I assume you can type? Yes? There's a computer and printer in the office through there." He points at another door. "You can start by writing a letter of resignation. After that, you can join me in the bedroom."

The Story Continues in 'The Master's Courtesan'

Part Three

The Master's Courtesan

I wake up in my dingy bedroom, and for a moment, I stare up in confusion at the ceiling, the events of the previous day swirling up inside me.

It seems unreal - fantastic but unreal. I shake my head. After meeting and having mind-blowing sex with a complete stranger, he offered me a job as his... his what? Courtesan? Call girl? And I accepted.

He *said* he owned the hotel. He said he owned a huge company. And I believed it all. Took it at face value.

My stomach churns. Things like this don't happen to girls like me. Was I taken in by some con man, after a quick roll with the maid?

I wrote a letter last night, resigning my old, horrible job cleaning at the hotel.

Oh my God! I resigned my job! What did I do with the letter?

Then I remember. It's still in *his* suite. I've not delivered it yet, so technically, I'm still working at the hotel, and due to start my shift again this afternoon.

I shake my head. Can it be real? The whole of the previous day feels surreal to me - from my foolish decision to use the stranger's shower, to the mind-boggling sex, when he found me there, naked in his bathroom.

I haul myself out of bed and set about making some coffee and toast. My head doesn't work in the morning until I have coffee inside me.

The intercom buzzes. "Delivery for Elizabeth Kimberley."

I buzz back. "Just leave it in the pigeonhole."

"Sorry. Needs a signature."

"Okay, I'm coming down."

What could it be? Am I expecting anything? I shake my head, trying to think if I have perhaps ordered something on the internet and forgotten about it. Not very likely on my very limited budget.

The courier is waiting in the tatty lobby, with its peeling paint and the smell of dampness. In fact, he has two items for me, a letter and a package. Puzzled, I sign for them and take them back to my apartment. Opening the letter first, I take a deep breath as I read the contents on Haswell Corporation letterhead.

Dear Miss Kimberley,

We are pleased to inform you that your application for an internship with our company has been accepted.

Please report to our offices...

I read on, catching my breath as I do so at the stated salary, which is much, much more than I earn now in my miserable cleaning job. Then I do a double take. I am being instructed to report to the offices this afternoon!

My eyes drift to the parcel. With slightly trembling fingers, I open it to find a skirt and jacket, blouses, and a pair of shoes, all very sensible and business-like, but beautifully made and expensive looking. I check the labels and take a deep breath. These designer brands cost a fortune. I would never be able to buy them myself.

I try them on, smoothing down the gorgeous slinky fabric over my curves. Looking at myself in my cracked mirror, I have to admit, the outfit looks great, and not quite as sensible as I had first thought. The jacket is tightly tailored to my trim waist and large breasts. The blouse is cut just low enough to suggest cleavage without actually revealing anything. The shoes have just enough of a heel to show off my legs, and the skirt, whilst at a business-like knee-length, is cut with a sexy swirl at the hem.

I love it. Obviously, it is a gift from him, but how did he know my size? For that matter, how did he know my address to have them delivered?

I check the time. I have two hours before I must report for my new job. I gulp down my coffee. A little low-key makeup and my long red hair confined into an orderly bun, and I feel ready to take on the world.

*****

Arriving at the Haswell Corporation office building, all steel and plate glass, I hand over the letter at the reception. The receptionist checks my name against a daybook and directs me to the tenth floor, where I find a second reception desk, with a pleasant-looking woman sitting behind it.

Again, I hold out the letter. "Hello, my name is Elizabeth Kimberley. I was told to report here."

The woman smiles. "Ah, yes, Miss Kimberley. Mr Haswell is expecting you. I'll tell him you're here."

She buzzes through on an intercom. "Mr Haswell, Elizabeth Kimberley for you."

"Thank you, Francis," replies the voice I came to know so well yesterday, under such unusual circumstances. "I'll just be five minutes. Please ask her to take a seat."

Francis points me to a row of low chairs and, gesturing to a coffee thermos on a low table, she says, "Make yourself comfortable, Miss Kimberley. Do help yourself to some coffee." But I am feeling too nervous already to want more coffee now.

After a short time, the intercom buzzes. "Francis, please show her in."

"Come with me." She smiles. "It's just through here."

Francis leads me through, taps on a door, and then after a moment opens it. "Miss Kimberley for you, sir." Then she leaves, pulling the door closed behind her.

The room is a wide-open office; one wall is entirely glass and overlooks the stunning cityscape far below. Neutral colours and minimalist decor only accentuate a large desk in a beautiful polished timber, walnut perhaps. I do not study it, because behind the desk, sits Richard Haswell.

He rises, smiling. In a dark suit, white shirt, tie, and immaculately polished shoes, his slightly greying hair contrasts against deeply tanned skin and piercingly blue eyes. Ye gods, but he is handsome. And that smile makes me melt inside, as I remember the same smile the night before.

"Ah, Elizabeth, good to see you again. Have a seat." He waves me to a couch overlooking the amazing vista. "Coffee?"

"Please, yes." Still a little anxious, not knowing quite what is expected of me, perhaps some caffeine pumping through my bloodstream might help. We have a contract, this man and I, and so far, he is fulfilling his end of it perfectly. Does he expect me to perform my end of it *here?*

He buzzes through, "Francis, coffee for two, please." Then he looks at me, perhaps divining my confusion. "Don't worry, Elizabeth. Here and now, in this place, you are a trainee, an intern. Your other duties come *later.*"

I smile nervously and nod my head.

"The suit looks good on you. I see I got the sizes right."

"It's lovely. Thank you."

"You're welcome, Elizabeth, but it is not simply a gift. Working here, you are representing my corporation, and I cannot have my representatives looking like, forgive me, but looking like hotel cleaners. Those clothes you were wearing last night, while well-chosen I'm sure on your limited budget, are not the kind of clothes I want my people to be seen in."

"However," and he smiles again, arching his brows, "there will be others. Some should be waiting for you when you get home. I expect you to wear them when you visit me this evening."

There is a tap at the door; Francis silently enters with a tray bearing a coffee pot and two cups, sets it down on the coffee table and just as silently, departs.

I gulp, then ask, "How did you know my address to send the things?"

"I asked the driver I sent you home with last night to make a note of it, and aren't you forgetting? You wrote your resignation letter on my laptop. Your address was on the letter too." He hesitates. "That's not a good address, Elizabeth. Not a safe place for a single girl to live." He pauses. "I am assuming you *are* single? No jealous husband out there?"

I shake my head.

"Boyfriend?"

I shake my head again. "I've been working so hard. My job and my studies..."

He nods in satisfaction. "Of course. Good. That's one potential problem dealt with then. Now... and I must ask you this..." He leans forward, closer to me. "Are you still happy with our arrangement? You need to tell me."

I nod, my mouth a little dry. "Yes, you've done everything you promised so far. I'll keep my end of the bargain."

He nods his head in approval. "Perfect answer, Elizabeth. Yes, I always keep my promises, and I deliver my end of any agreement. It's good to know that you see it that way too."

"Won't people think it a bit odd that I suddenly appear like this? Out of the blue? It's not as though I had an interview or anything."

He laughs. "I think you did rather well at your *interview* last night, Elizabeth. As for people thinking it odd, no, they won't. I have a number of employees who I met outside of normal channels and have offered them a job."

He sees my expression and laughs. "No, not quite like you and I met, and no, not with the same agreement. But, Francis out there, for example, my personal assistant, I met her on a train. She was reading the business pages of her newspaper, quite unusual in a woman, if you don't mind me saying so. We started talking about her views on equities and a city merger that was coming up. She was working as a waitress - all that potential going to waste. I hired her on the spot. A good personal assistant needs to understand the business of her employer. So, no, don't worry, the staff here know that I choose employees for my own reasons."

I am feeling more reassured. "So, what happens now?"

"Francis will take you to HR. They'll take you through the usual formalities, and then we'll put you through the usual intern routine. You will spend time in every department of the company: finance, procurement, marketing, everything. You will see the whole machine, and we can find out how much you already know and see where you can fit in best."

He leans back in his seat, holding me with his eyes. "Now, about your other duties - when you finish here for the day, you will go home and put on the clothes you will find waiting for you. Wear your hair up, as you have it now. I expect to see you in my suite at eight o'clock. Any questions?"

"Um, I'm not sure what to call you."

He laughs. "Here, I am Mr Haswell. When I take you out to dinner, I am Richard. In my apartment, you will call me Master. Understood?"

"Yes, Mr Haswell."

"Finish your coffee." He buzzes the intercom again. "Francis, can you take Elizabeth to HR please?"

The rest of the day passes in a blur as I sign my contract of employment, am introduced to people, shown my office, and talked through rules and procedures. By five-thirty I am exhausted, my head is spinning, and I am ready to go home. I am eager too, to see what is waiting for me.

There are a number of parcels waiting for me in the tatty lobby. Dashing up to my room, I open them with trembling anticipation.

There is a pair of shoes, black satin with impossibly high heels; they are beautiful but not intended for actually walking in. Richard is tall, but standing whilst wearing them, I might be taller. Or perhaps not, as he is well over six feet. And, I reflect, we are all the same height lying down...

There are also stockings and underwear, mainly in black, but some in red and others in white. A bodice, with long silk laces dangling invitingly. A skirt, with a long slit up the side, in a far more daring cut than I would normally wear. Another skirt, this one a wraparound style, and I notice it's cut for *easy access*. The list goes on, and I am dazzled at suddenly having so many beautiful things.

I cannot wear them all, and so I take my time, trying them on, in turn, twisting this way and that, trying to see myself from all angles in the stained mirror. Eventually, I make my choice, adding only a small necklace from my own things - a glass dewdrop on a silver chain. I take a long dark coat to cover my outfit.

I do not want to walk through the dark streets, and with my new and gloriously high salary, I can afford a taxi. At the hotel, I spot Ricardo at the reception desk.

Damn.

This could be embarrassing.

I decide to be brazen and simply walk to take the lift, behaving as though I have every right to do so. Then it dawns on me. I *do* have every right to do so. I have been invited. I cross the lobby, only to hear Ricardo's voice behind me.

"Excuse me, madam. That's a private lift. The main lift for the hotel is over there." I turn to see him pointing, then recognition dawns across his face and his polite *talk to the guests* face turns into a scowl. "Beth! What the fuck do you think you're doing? First, you don't turn up to work, and then you march in hours late as though you owned the place?"

Words stick in my throat. I wrote my resignation letter. Surely Richard would have given it to the hotel manager?

"Mr Chambers is fucking furious with you. He told me to send you down to the office if you turned up."

What do I say? I have no idea, so I settle for the truth. "I'm sorry, Ricardo, and please tell Mr Chambers so, but I'll have to talk to him later. I have an appointment upstairs now."

"The fuck you do! Get your ass into the office. I'll tell Mr Chambers that you're here."

I don't know what to do. "Ricardo, I'll come back to explain, but right now I have to go." And I walk back to the lift, pressing the up button.

Ricardo is talking on the phone. I overhear some of it. "...don't know what the fuck she thinks she's doing..." and as he finishes speaking, Mr Chambers, my old boss, stomps into the lobby.

"What is all this about? Beth, you didn't turn up to work today. Where were you? And what do you think you're doing trying to take the penthouse lift?"

His face changes as he registers my appearance and how I am dressed. "What's this then? Get your lazy butt..."

The reception phone rings and Ricardo picks it up. "Good evening, Hotel Haswell. How can I help you? Oh, yes, Mr Haswell... Yes?" His eyes cross over to me. "Yes, sir, she's here. We were just having a little chat. Yes, I'll send her right up."

He puts the phone down and looks me up and down. "Got our feet right under the table, haven't we?" he says, his voice dripping venom. "Go on then. Off you go. Mr Haswell wants to see you." His lip curls.

Unnerved, but determined not to show it, I lift my head high and take the lift to the penthouse.

*****

I knock on the door and Richard Haswell, billionaire owner of one of the largest corporations in the world, *my Master*, opens the suite door, inviting me in with an outstretched arm. Inside, he takes my coat, slipping it from my shoulders, and hanging it carefully in a closet. Dressed casually again, he wears a loose white linen shirt and tight black jeans.

He leans in to kiss me, looking closely at my face. "Are you all right, Elizabeth? You seem upset."

I nod, not wanting to discuss what has just happened. "I'm fine. It's nothing."

He holds my gaze, clearly not believing me, but then changes the subject. "Have you eaten? Are you hungry?"

"Err, yes, I'm hungry. Actually, I didn't eat," I say. Then flushing, I add, "I was excited by all the lovely things you sent. Thank you."

He smiles, nodding in acknowledgement. "You're welcome, Elizabeth, and I see you have used them well. Come over here into the light. I want to see you." He leads me to stand by the window, then sits in an armchair, looking at me. "Turn around. Let me look at you."

A little self-consciously, I turn around under his fixed gaze. I am wearing a simple blouse, very low-cut that shows off my cleavage. The teardrop pendant dangles between my breasts. The wraparound skirt, tight on my trim waist, flares out, silky and sensuous over my long legs. I pull the skirt slightly to one side, showing my Master one stocking covered thigh.

He sits, head on one hand, propped on the chair arm, just watching, drinking me in. He looks simply astonishing, dark-haired and dark-eyed as he gazes on, his beautifully chiselled features fixed on me. He is my Master now, but I have never felt so powerful, so *alive.*

"You look beautiful, Elizabeth."

I flush again, unsure now of his wishes.

"Unbutton your blouse," he says, "Slowly." Then seeing my eyes glance at the window, he adds, "It's mirrored glass. No one can see in. *Now,* unbutton your blouse."

My Master expects to be obeyed, and so, one by one, I slip the buttons free, until the silken garment hangs loosely from my shoulders, my full breasts protruding beyond the folds.

"Take it off." Obediently, I let the blouse slide to the ground where it ripples onto the thick, soft carpet. My bra, chosen to enhance my cleavage, is black satin, matching the thong I am wearing. I start to take off the bra, but he says, "No. Come here." And compliantly, I approach.

I feel incredibly erotic. My total surrender of will to this man's wishes is arousing something in me, which, until only the previous day, I had not suspected in myself. I warm from within, embers of arousal beginning to fan into flame.

"Closer. I want to be able to touch you, to smell you."

As I stand over him, he reaches into the folds of the skirt, pulling the fabric back in a train behind me, exposing the thong panties along with my stockings. His hands continue their journey behind me to the tops of my thighs, gathering me in and pulling me close, his face against my stomach as he kisses and nibbles my skin. Then, one hand still clasping me from behind, with a single finger he slides inside the front of my panties, pulling them slightly to one side, and lowering his head, nuzzling his face against me.

I can feel his hot breath against me as he softly bites at my skin. My breathing quickens, and he smiles as he hears it. "Good girl, Elizabeth. That's right. I'll have you screaming soon enough, but you have to earn it."

He laps slowly at my sex, tongue exploring, then says, "Part your legs. Spread your thighs for me."

He slides two fingers between my legs, over my bud, and towards my pussy, stroking gently, fondling my clit, massaging my pussy lips. I begin to gasp, and I stagger slightly as my body reacts to the oh-so-gentle stimulation he is giving me, waves of arousal fanning over me.

"Did I say you could move?"

I shake my head. "No, I'm sorry. It's not easy to stand still when you're doing that."

He glances up into my eyes. "Is that so? We'd better do something about it then."

In a swift change of mood, grabbing my wrists, he pulls me into the bedroom and pushes me roughly back against a wall. Hand hard on me, flat between my breasts, he simply says, "Stay."

On a side table, there are several items laid out: vibes, ropes, dildos, handcuffs...

He selects the cuffs. Snapping them onto my wrists, he says, "What's it to be? Stretched up or bending over?"

I don't know what to say, so with my heart beginning to race, I say nothing.

"Silent again, Elizabeth? Let's see what we can do to change that."

Grabbing my arms roughly, he raises my arms above my head, to where I notice for the first time, a hook in the wall. Attaching the cuffs to the hook, he produces the spreader bar I saw the night before, cuffing in first one ankle, and then the other. He pulls the pins from my hair, and it cascades down over my breasts to my waist, a tumble of auburn waves.

He stands back to admire his handiwork and then shakes his head. Kneeling, he adjusts the bar, pushing it and my ankles wider. "Spread your legs. I want you *open.*" His voice is harsh, intense.

It is difficult to move at all, and as I try to obey, I totter, all my weight on my wrists for a moment. From his kneeling position, my Master forces my ankles farther apart, and farther, until I can barely stand at all, my wrists taking the strain. He unwraps my legs from the folds of the skirt, tucking the fabric behind me.

"That's better," he says. "Now we have you properly presented."

Standing back, he starts to strip, his eyes never leaving mine as he removes his shirt. I am entranced by his tight, lean muscled body, by the dark line of hair leading from his navel to his belt and below. Broad-shouldered and tight waisted, I want nothing more than for him to fuck me stupid. His black jeans, previously a perfect fit, are straining at the front, and as he unbelts and unzips, his manhood stands upright against him, firm against his flat stomach. I watch, hypnotised by his beautiful physique, staring at his erection.

He follows my stare and grins. "Like what you see, Elizabeth? Don't worry, it's all going to be inside you. I'm just deciding where."

Coming close, he lifts my breasts from the confines of the lacy bra, cupping and kneading each in turn. He tweaks at the nipples, raising them to hard brown buds, then bends to suckle one, whilst pinching and squeezing the other, sending electric waves of arousal through my core to my pussy.

My breathing is so heavy now, so fast, and moisture is running down my skin, from the sweat of my rising heat, and from my pussy, now flowing freely down my legs. He looks at me, eyes lingering on my breasts, my flat belly, the parting of my legs.

"Too many clothes," he says, grasping the skirt at the waist and tugging. With a pop of buttons and a rip of fabric, it tears free. I start to protest, but roughly he grabs my chin, turning my face to his. "No!" he says, then, more gently, "I'll buy you another one."

The ragged cloth of the beautiful skirt is cast to one side. And next, he reaches for my panties, pulling and tearing, ripping them off me.

I am still wearing the bra and stockings. "You can keep those on," he says, then kisses me fiercely. There is nothing tender or gentle here. His mouth is hard on my lips, forcing my mouth open.

He drops to his knees, face up close, pulling my pussy lips apart and wrapping his tongue around my clit, working it mercilessly.

I moan, trying to struggle, but I have nowhere to go. Cuffed hand and foot, legs spread, and with my all my weight resting on my wrists, I *cannot* move. I can only writhe helplessly against the cascade of sensation. With his tongue working my clit, he slips fingers into my pussy and rubs hard against my inner walls. I can hear nothing, feel nothing, except the pain of my wrists and the inescapable pleasure, pain, delight, and torment of my Master's tongue and fingers. My moaning increases, turning to squeals, fighting against the breathlessness of my rapid breathing.

My heart pounding, a climax wells up inside, and my squeals turn into a triumphant scream as my orgasm pulses through me, pounding through my pussy, belly, and thighs. My legs give out from under me, and I hang by my wrists, writhing and shaking, helpless in the grip of my crashing climax.

I do not hang for long. Before the spasm passes, my Master rises, unhooks the handcuffs from the wall and propels me to the bed. Hobbled by the bar, legs asplay, I can barely move, and he picks me up, depositing me roughly kneeling facedown over the bed.

My legs spread-eagled by the bar, my pink and swollen sex is open and displayed to him as he kneels behind me, and with one hand on my back pinning me down, he thrusts his shaft hard into me.

He is huge, and at almost any other time, I would struggle to accommodate him, but in my state of screaming arousal, he sheathes himself, full-length, straight into my dripping passage, pounding into me.

I scream again, and an orgasm wells up once more, my pussy walls grasping and gripping as they throb around him.

His hand leaves my back and I feel him grasping me by the waist, forcing me back and forth against his rhythm, heightening the drive of his shaft, intensifying his already deep thrusting as he rams into me, plunging into my depths.

Through my own cries, I hear him moan and gasp, feel the pulsing of his cock spurting into me. For moments, he holds, shuddering against me, then relaxes down with a gasp.

For half a minute, he simply lies on top of me spent, before taking a couple of deep breaths then kissing the back of my neck. "That was good, Elizabeth. Thank you." He pulls away, moving to unshackle me.

He throws me a white terry cloth robe and puts one on himself. "Ready to eat?" he asks.

I suddenly realise I am starving. "Oh, yes, I am."

"We'll have something sent up. Order what you want. I'll have a steak, rare."

I order the same for myself, slightly self-conscious to be asking for service from people I was working with only the day before.

"What happened downstairs in the lobby, Elizabeth? You looked upset as you came in."

"I'd forgotten to give them my letter of resignation," I said sheepishly. "They wanted to know why the maid was taking the private lift to the penthouse."

He looks me in the eyes. "You didn't forget. It was here. I'm sure you assumed that I would pass it along. In fact, I had realised that it is not appropriate."

Confused, I shake my head.

He continues. "You haven't resigned. You've simply been promoted. Yesterday, you were just as much my employee as today. I own this hotel, remember? You are simply working under a different contract."

My Master takes my chin in his hand, kissing my forehead. "I'm sorry if I caused you embarrassment. I should have thought to let them know down there. I was thinking of you in other ways..."

He is apologising to *me?*

He wiggles his eyebrows at me and winks, and I laugh.

"Now," he continues, "a break, I think, for some rest and refreshments."

A *break?* And then?

There is a knock at the door. "Room service."

He smiles at me. "Ah, perfect timing." Then he calls out, "Leave it there."

Turning back to me, he says, "I'll make sure that things are settled with your *previous* manager. For now, I don't see the need for you to meet any of the other staff."

He waits a moment, then opens the door, bringing in a trolley bearing our meals, plus champagne on ice and strawberries and cream.

An hour later, with the food eaten, and a glass or two inside me, I am lying on the fur rug in front of the fire, eating strawberries dipped in champagne and cream, reveling in the sheer luxury of it all. I notice that my Master, who is sitting on the couch, has only drunk a little of the champagne, and is watching me closely.

As I dip each bright red berry in the wine and then the cream, I pass it, still dripping, to my mouth, sucking it gradually through my lips.

It dawns on me that I am giving a performance, so I take my time, locking my eyes with his as I lick and suck the creamy champagne from the fruit. I see the approval in his eyes as, one at a time, I slowly consume each fruit.

He watches as I caress each strawberry with my tongue, licking it clean of the dripping cream before gently biting in and swallowing.

He stands up, towering over me, lying at his feet. "On your knees, Elizabeth."

I obey. Looking up at my Master, it is clear what I am being instructed to do. I rise to kneel before him, untying the belt of his robe and opening it to expose his already hard cock.

Only an hour ago, this man came explosively inside me, and yet now, his erection stands proud once again.

"I've not had a shower yet, Elizabeth. Lick me clean."

I lean forward to kiss away the drop of pre-cum already glistening at the tip, sucking my lips at the combined salty and sweet flavour of him. Then I start to lick slowly at the head of his shaft, tracing its contours with my tongue, exploring and probing with the tip. I feel my Master shudder and hear his gasp.

His voice is hoarse as he orders me. "All of it, Elizabeth."

Compliantly, I lick the full length of his shaft, starting at the base and drawing long slow strokes up his massive, throbbing member. His breathing turns ragged, and he starts to flow, as do I. My slit is wet again, and juices trickle inside my thighs to my knees.

He grasps my head, winding my hair tight around his fingers. "Open your mouth."

I do so, wondering how much of his length I can take - certainly not all of it, but he says huskily, "Use your hands as well."

Fastening my lips around him, I use my hands to take much of his length. My saturated slit is running freely with pussy juices, and I use some on my hands, to make the grip I have on him slippery and pleasurable.

His breathing is patchy, and looking up, I see him looking back down at me, watching as his cock slides in and out of my mouth.

With my lips, I give him as tight of a grip as I can, and with my hands, I feel his tension build. His balls tighten and harden, his musky scent growing stronger as his flow increases.

I taste his essence filling my mouth, and then, with a groan, he grabs my head firmly, pinning me and thrusting hard into my mouth.

My hands prevent him from filling my throat, but as he spurts, I gag, his cum hitting the back of my throat. His pelvis flexes and bucks as he shoots into me and cum dribbles from my lips, dripping onto my breasts.

As he relaxes, he pulls my head back, withdrawing from me a little and turning my face upwards. "Don't even think about spitting," he says, his eyes intense as he watches me lick my lips clean and swallow his cream.

He reaches down, and with one finger, he wipes the cum from my breasts and holds his finger to my mouth. "Finish it." And I lick his finger clean.

"Good girl," he says approvingly. "Now, finish your strawberries."

The Story Continues in 'The Master's Desires'

Part Four
The Master's Desires

I am lying on a bed, blindfolded and with my arms stretched wide above my head, chained to the bedposts.

I am wearing very little - a silky black camisole, stockings with black lacy tops, and a matching thong, which, right now, is doing little except act as a partial barrier to my flooding pussy.

My legs are spread, and kneeling between them I think, although I cannot be sure because I cannot see or even move very well, is Richard Haswell, billionaire owner of one of the largest corporations in the country, perhaps the world. My Master.

Two weeks ago, I didn't have anything. I was an almost penniless student doing dead-end work to make ends meet. Now, I have an amazing job, am receiving top-class training so that I will one day be qualified and independent in my own right, am showered with beautiful clothes, wined and dined, and taken to amazing places. And for all this, all I have to do is give my Master whatever he wants, whenever he wants it.

I think he is still clothed. I feel the smooth fabric of his tight cut black jeans rubbing against my open thighs, his erection pressed against my stomach.

His lips are suckling on my left nipple; his tongue is manipulating and kneading it, sending electric currents of desire shockingly down through my stomach, hips, and aching cunt.

He switches to the other nipple, and forcing my legs farther apart with his knees, he arranges me to his satisfaction. His hot breath on the sensitive skin of my breasts is making me flush and sweat. I feel his tongue trail along my cleavage, licking me dry. My breath is rapid and shallow, and as his tongue rides back to a nipple, he bites, not hard, but enough to startle me and I half gasp, half yelp at the almost pain of his nip.

"No noise, Elizabeth," he says. "This time, I want you silent." Then he bites the other nipple. Arching my back and shuddering, I try to obediently be silent through my panting.

One hand slides across my breast, pinching the nipple and then tweaking and teasing until I know that it is a solid, erect bud, crinkling rose against my Celtic pale skin.

My other nipple gets the same treatment, and I writhe under him, my hips beginning to judder with the need to have him inside me. So far, he has touched only my breasts, belly, and neck, not yet venturing near my streaming pussy and swollen clit.

"What do you want, Elizabeth?" he asks in his deep, rich voice.

What does he expect me to say? I want him to plant his mouth over my slit and suck me dry. I want him to fuck me until I can't stand. But all I can do is moan incoherently.

*****

Earlier that day, having been sent to his office with some documents for his attention, he waves me to a seat. "Sit down, Elizabeth. I just wanted a brief chat. Bear with me, I won't be but a moment."

Quickly, he scans the documents, then signing one, he passes the file back to me. "Thanks. Give those back to Mack and tell him I'd like to see the two-year forecasts as well."

I make a quick note of this. Mack, Micale Kane, manager of the procurement section, is my immediate supervisor for the moment, while I spend a couple of weeks in procurement. As part of my internship program with the company, I learn what each department does, how it works, and where it fits in the scheme of things.

I don't care for the man. His smile always seems fake to me, and while he hasn't tried to make a move on me, there is something about him that always makes me want to wash my hands after I've been talking to him.

Of course, I have said none of this to Richard. I am the new kid on the block, and even with our *special arrangement,* I am sure that it would not be well-received if I started mouthing off about people who have been here for years.

"So, how's the training going?"

Pulling back my attention to where it belongs, I reply, "Great. It's so interesting. Being able to link up what they teach us at college with how a company actually works in practice..."

"And the college? Your studies?"

"Oh, it's all fine now. HR got me onto a day release program, with three days a week here and two in college. I can cover all the bases this way - get to grips with the things I need to learn, both on paper and for real."

He nods in satisfaction. "Good. And you *are* getting to grips with things? Where are you now, for example? Procurement, is it?"

I nod. "Yes, I'm working my way through. I haven't got my head around all of it yet, but I'll get there."

"Something's giving you problems? What is it?"

I am reluctant to ask him a lot of questions. This is, after all, Richard Haswell. Billionaire tycoons have better things to do than answer questions from half-cocked trainees.

"C'mon," he says. "Out with it." He glances at the clock. "I have fifteen minutes before my next meeting, so ask."

"Err, well, I am learning my way around the procurement process and trying to tie up in my head where the paperwork fits in with the computer system..."

"And?"

"Well, I can't figure it out. It is just so complicated with all the different projects you have going on, and in so many different places, so I decided to just pick one project, as a kind of working example, and follow the paper trail."

Nodding his head, he says, "Good idea. So?"

"Well, I picked the Hanover Mall project you've got going on over at the other side of the city. And I just can't get it to work in my head when I try to fit the pieces together. I keep coming back in a loop and finding myself at the same place again. It is like the same things are being charged twice or even more than twice. I don't get it at all."

I shrug. "Certainly, that can't be it and I'm probably missing something really obvious..." My voice trails off. I feel nervous that I'm making a fool of myself in front of this man who has given me the opportunity of a lifetime.

He nods thoughtfully, pursing his lips. "As you say, you are probably missing something. Print me off a copy of what you've got and bring it over tonight. I'll take a look at it for you. Meanwhile..." he looks at me meaningfully, "... speaking of tonight - seven o'clock?"

I cast my eyes down "Yes, Sir."

He sucks in his cheeks, smiling. "Elizabeth, don't do that here. I can't attend meetings with a raging hard-on."

Lost for words, I bob a curtsey. "Yes, Mr Haswell." And I go about my business.

*****

Later that evening, I am sure he does have a raging hard-on. While I can't see it, I can feel it pressing against my thighs as he leans into me.

"What do you want, Elizabeth? This won't go any further until you ask me for it."

I hear a buzz, then feel a sharp pain in one nipple, then the other, as he clamps vibes to my small, firm buttons.

This is too much, and I struggle against the chains, trying to escape the electric arousal spiking through me. My pussy gushes and I moan, trying to thrash both against and into the sensation.

"What do you want, Elizabeth? Tell me. You have to tell me."

"I want... I want..."

"Yes?"

"Oh, God! I want you inside me. Please. I want you inside me."

"That's better. And then?"

I am half-crazy with lust. I can barely think straight. "I want you to fuck me. Please, just fuck me."

"That's good, Elizabeth. And how do you want to be fucked?"

I am not sure how to answer and hesitate, my panting growing ragged.

"How do you want to be fucked, Elizabeth? Tongue? Fingers? Or do I get myself balls-deep inside you, and pin your pretty brains to your skull?"

The image this question conjures up is too much, and I moan again. It is about the only thing I can do, bound and blindfolded.

"Enough noise, Elizabeth. If you can't ask nicely for what you want, I think I'll shut you up." His fingers prise my mouth open, forcing something inside and then tying around at the back of my head. A ball of some kind? It is soft and rubbery against my tongue, but my mouth is held open against it. I am effectively gagged, and now my helpless moans are muffled.

"You look good like that, Elizabeth, with your mouth held open. I might have to think about what else I might put in there. But for now, a little more stimulation, I think," he says.

After a moment, I again feel a sharp pain in first one nipple and then the other. I try to yelp, but cannot. Then, my already sensitive nipples start to vibrate, gently at first. I am just beginning to handle this exquisite sensation when the vibe increases violently. I convulse, my hips bucking, my urgent cries blocked by my gag. I try to speak, but cannot.

"Too late now, Elizabeth. You had your chance to speak."

He lifts my left leg by the knee, passing something under it. A rope? A belt? A cuff? Blinded as I am, I cannot tell. Then he does the same with my right knee. Abruptly, I find both legs being spread, parted at the knees, lifting me from the hip and displaying my throbbing pussy. For a moment, my weight is suspended quite painfully as my knees are pulled back and towards my face, but then he pushes something under my hips, a pillow or cushion supporting me and the pain subsides.

I lie, almost crucified on the bed, blindfolded, gagged, arms chained, and legs bent almost doubled back on themselves, with my pussy splayed.

"Not quite wide enough, I think," comes my Master's voice. And the ropes pull my knees farther apart. He adjusts the cushion under my hips, forcing my back to arch, pushing my hips higher, and my dripping pussy is now even more exposed. "That's better, Elizabeth. Now I can see you properly."

I am so ready for him. Frantic with arousal, crazy with lust, I just want him to plunge his cock inside me and pound away at my core.

Instead, I feel the lightest of touches. Fingers part my pussy lips, stretching them wide. His face is so close to me. I feel his warm breath over my swollen and pulsating labia, then his tongue curls around them, over and around, continuing on to my pussy where he pushes in, licking me inside. The pressure of his face against me tells me he is licking as deep as he is able, probing with the tip and tasting my juices. His whole mouth fastens around me, and he starts chewing at me, his tongue working me all the time as I heave and struggle and squeal against my bonds, the gag, and the exquisite pleasure and pain of it all. I try to scream against the ball gag in my mouth, but it fights against me, and only muffled cries escape.

Then he withdraws, leaving me shaking and shuddering, hips jerking and bucking against my ties. My pussy is hot, drenched, engorged, and I am desperate to have him inside me.

He removes the gag. "Anything to say, Elizabeth?" he asks. "Any requests yet? You know you have to ask first."

My mouth is dry from the gag, and my jaw is aching from being held open, so I have trouble speaking. "Inside me. Please, Master, inside me."

"That's better, Elizabeth. You are learning nicely. I'll take your training a little further after today."

I barely have time to wonder what he means by this when he slips something inside me. Sliding easily against my slick pussy lips, he inserts something, which for a moment, simply sits inside me. Then it also starts to vibrate to a pulsing rhythm. An egg?

I convulse again, but still, I am pinned.

"Calm down, Elizabeth. We've barely started." He probes with a finger inside me, pushing the vibe in deeper, pressing it in as far as it will go. "Now, Elizabeth, I want to hear you yelp for me." He turns the power up, and this time, the part-moan, part-howl that comes from me is loud and long. Mercilessly, he wraps his mouth around my clit, sucking hard at my swollen bud. I struggle and wriggle, trying to escape the sensation overload, but at the same time, glorying in it.

The combination of vibration on my nipples, pulsing from within, and his mouth clamped over me, is tormenting and pleasuring me and is irresistible.

From within, an orgasm swells and rises, building to the peak, and then in an uncontrollable surge, takes me. My Master works my clit with his tongue, drinking me as I gush, one hand on my flat belly, massaging my inner muscles against the egg. I scream against the unbearable, sweet, bitter, pleasure, and pain that overwhelms me completely.

"Stop! Stop! Oh, God, please stop!"

Instantly, he takes his mouth away. Inserting fingers, he flicks the egg out of me, then tugs the clamps off my nipples. The blindfold is ripped from my face, and in the shimmer of the candlelight, I see my Master, shirtless and undoing his straining belt. Unbuttoning his jeans, his erection bulges from the fabric, standing upright as he releases it, rigid against him.

He climbs onto the bed, settling between my knees, the tip of his penis kissing my pussy lips, still twitching in the aftershock of my orgasm. As he touches me, my inner muscles convulse again at the thought of this thick shaft penetrating me.

"Watch me, Elizabeth," he says and obediently, I look up into his face.

"No," he says. "There." His eyes point down to where his massive cock is brushing my entrance. "Watch me, Elizabeth. Watch me fucking your cunt."

I drop my gaze, and he leans in, pushing slowly inside me. An inch. Two inches. Four inches. His thick shaft, wide against my pussy, stretching me open, penetrates slowly and I tremble.

He breathes deeply and says, "That's good, Elizabeth. That's really good. Keep watching."

Briefly, my eyes flick up to his.

"Down! Remember what you're looking at."

His own hips quiver, and then with a gasp, he plunges the rest of the way inside me, his balls banging against me. Almost instantly, my climax starts to gather again, and I moan and then yell as he pounds inside me to a slow rhythm. Deliberately, he times each stroke, and I watch as he thrusts his cock deep into my core, my pussy welcoming him as he bangs into me hard.

Again and again, I watch as he sheathes himself in me, thrusting in deep as far as he can go against my inner walls. I gasp and quake, but bound as I am, all I can do is shake, quiver, and scream. I fling my head back, wanting to scream up to the ceiling, but he grabs the back of my head. With his fingers twisting through my long red hair, he pulls me forward. "Watch, I said!" he says fiercely. "I want you to watch me fucking you."

I look as his cock fucks my slick pussy. Then, with a deep intake of breath, he shudders against me, pumping his load into me, and grasping onto the ropes restraining my knees as he climaxes inside me.

For a moment, he remains still, his chest heaving and his skin glistening with sweat. Finally pulling himself upright, he looks me in the eyes and grins. As he unbuckles the cuffs from my knees, he says, "You're quite a woman, Elizabeth." With both hands, he sweeps his sweaty hair back over his head. Then he looks at me. "Have you eaten?"

"Er, no. With you asking me to come a bit earlier, I didn't..."

"Would you like to go out to dinner?"

Would I?

On the arm of this amazing man?

"I'd love to, but I've nothing to wear. I can't go out in public wearing what I arrived in." I'm sure the taxi driver had my number, or at least X-ray vision, when I wore just a long coat over my undies.

He waves that off. "Yes, you do. Look in there," he says, pointing at one of the wardrobes. "I have prepared for this eventuality, and you will find plenty to choose from in there. Pick something... demure, but accessible."

I begin to see where this is going. "What kind of place are we going to?"

He thinks for a minute. "Courtney's, I think. The management there know me and the staff are well paid to be discreet about their diners." He waves me towards the wardrobe. "Pick out your clothes. I'm going for a shower."

I know of Courtney's. It is well-known as a hangout for celebrities, from rock stars to politicians, actors to newspaper tycoons - public faces who value a bit of privacy from time to time. It also has a reputation for being stupendously expensive.

My Master leaves me, like a kid in a candy store, investigating the wardrobe, working my way through beautiful fabrics, expensive designer labels and gorgeous *fuck me* dresses.

All the clothes are beautiful, stylish, and well-chosen, with a good mix of themes and styles, but as I work my way through them, it dawns on me what the common themes are. Firstly, they are all just my size...

How does he ***do*** *that?*

Secondly, every one of them, in some way, is *easy access.* The lovely garments might be demure on the surface, but every one of them has some form of flap, wrap, slit, lace, or button that would allow an experienced hand an easy way in.

I pick out a cocktail dress with a tightly fitted bodice, but a loose, flaring skirt. The filmy fabric swirls as I lift it up to admire before I lay it carefully on the bed and head off to shower myself.

Showered, made up, and dressed, I go through to the lounge, to find Richa - my Master - sitting; he is dressed and well-groomed and is looking through the file I brought. He glances up and then looks up again as he registers that I am dressed. He tilts his head admiringly. "Ready?"

"Yes, I think so."

"I think so too. You look beautiful, Elizabeth, but of course, you always do. Shall we go?" He stands, puts the file on the table, and offers me his arm.

*****

I walk into the restaurant on the arm of Richard Haswell. It is beautiful, with elaborate chandeliers and polished woodwork, and there is even a pianist playing softly in the background. The meal is to die for, perfectly cooked and exquisitely served.

My Master seems distracted. After seeing the clothes in the wardrobe, I had thought that perhaps he would want to make some kind of play in the car on the way here. Instead, whilst he slipped his hand inside the skirt, resting it on my inner thigh, he did not speak, he just simply looked out the window until, pulling up outside the restaurant, Ross, the driver, asked, "You want me to wait, Mr Haswell?"

"Yes, please, Ross. I'll call you when we're ready to leave."

Sitting at the table, with the wonderful food and wine being served, and a low murmur of conversation around us, he is silent. I had expected that since he has brought me out to dinner that he might want to talk.

I wonder if I have upset him somehow.

"Mr Haswell. Is something wrong? Have I... have I done something wrong?"

He almost jerks back to reality and smiles at me. "No, not at all, Elizabeth. I just have a lot to think about right now. I'm sorry. It's not very gracious of me to sit in silence. And also, here..." he takes my hand before continuing, "... here, in this place, in this setting, it is 'Richard.'"

Relief washes over me. "I was beginning to worry that I had upset you, Richard."

He leans close and kisses me on the forehead, cupping my face in his hands. "No, I am simply distracted. Please, do enjoy your meal. Is your fish good?"

"Yes, very." In fact, the fish is divine, with tender white flakes in a buttery sauce, piquant with capers and lemon, and served with tiny, bite-size vegetables, crisp and fresh, that taste as though they were still on the plant five minutes ago. The restaurant deserves its reputation and is a world away from the takeout pizza I was living on only a short time ago.

Later, Ross drives the car to my apartment to drop me off.

Richard almost growls when he sees where we are. "I don't like you living here, Elizabeth. It's not safe. I can understand why you lived here... in your previous life... you couldn't afford any better then, but it's different now. Why haven't you moved somewhere else?"

"Oh, I will. I have somewhere picked out, in fact. But I'm waiting for my first paycheck to come through. Then, trust me," I laugh. "I'll be out of here. They won't see me for dust."

"Of course, yes. That's good. Good night, Elizabeth." He kisses me as I step out of the car.

As I turn the key in the lock, I look back. The car is still there, and Ross and Richard are both looking at me. "Waiting for something?" I call.

Ross replies, "Always do, Beth." He tosses his head, pointing to the rear seats. "He's made it clear that if I don't stay long enough to see you in, he'll have my ass."

I chuckle. It's nice to know that someone will take the trouble to watch out for me. "That's great. Good night, Ross. Good night, Richard."

*****

In my dingy apartment, my good mood evaporates into a feeling of let-down. Why? I've had a wonderful evening, have been wined and dined, had sex that left me wanting to scrape the top of my head off the ceiling. Why do I suddenly feel blue? The food, so delicious, sits heavily inside me.

In my bed, I admit to myself that I'm lonely for him. I would like to be curled up in his bed with his arms around me as I drift off to sleep.

But that is not the deal we have. This is not a *relationship.* I am not his girlfriend or even a fuck buddy. I am an employee, simply one with some very good terms written into the agreement we made. I will have all the good things in life, including the training and education I need, to one day be rich and independent in my own right. For that, I *service* my Master, billionaire Richard Haswell.

I can't complain. It is the chance of a lifetime. Nonetheless, I wish for more.

I cannot sleep, finding myself thinking of my Master, of his face as he commands me with deep, deep blue eyes gazing at my breasts, my sex. I think of the obvious pleasure he takes in bringing me to crashing orgasms, of his beautiful body, lean and tanned in those linen shirts and tight black jeans that he prefers to wear.

He fucks me to a spectacular orgasm every time, but I am beginning to wish that he might, just once, make love to me.

Love. The forbidden word. It is not in the contract.

Oh, God...

Don't let me fall in love with him.

Almost instinctively, my hands drift south, and I sigh deeply as I open my legs, raising my knees, and parting my thighs to allow my fingers entry.

Simply opening myself is so erotic. I think of his eyes on me, watching closely as he commands me to spread myself open, stretch my pussy lips open to his inspection, to pleasure myself, to bring myself to climax, to fuck myself so that he can watch and enjoy, and to take me when he wishes, his fingers probing my fluid core, or his tongue licking long, slow strokes up through my glistening folds, delving deep or lightly, barely brushing skin.

I think of his eyes, dark in the glimmering candlelight, intense with desire, brilliant in lust, looking at me as he instructs me in his wishes. I am to have no secrets. He must see it all.

And I respond and obey, my arousal rising sweet and hot from within, under the power he has over me.

My fingers slide through my red curls, just re-growing after my Master shaved me that first day he discovered me illicitly using his shower.

I chuckle as I remember my reaction - hands tied above my head to his shower fitting, naked to his eyes, as he produced the razor and foam. He shaved me then tongued me to a quivering orgasm, before bending me over the basin and fucking me, balls-deep inside me, to his own climax.

He hasn't done anything like that since then, and with my fingers slipping past to my nub, I wonder if he would like me to wax. Does he want my pussy smooth and naked for him, so that he can see my slit, there for him, glistening with moisture as juices trickle down my thighs?

Does he prefer it now, sleek red hairs peeping through? Or perhaps he wants them to grow so that he can shave me again? My pussy juices are flowing at the thought of his mouth around me, sucking me. A flash of heat stabs up through my sex, and I feel my flow starting again, my slit swelling and my breath quickening.

I work my clit, rubbing and circling, slipping back the hood to reach the sensitive bud within. As I flick it, I think of his tongue encircling, probing with the tip, exploring my pink folds, lapping slowly at my pussy juices, tasting me as he slides fingers inside me and probes me within.

My heart begins to pound, and I wish that I had one of the vibes he uses on me so expertly. I want to feel something inside me, so with one hand still plying my swelling nub, the other slides inside, one finger, two, then three. I want *him* inside me, but this will have to do.

I reach in and up, stretching fingers for my G-spot, massaging hard, and for a moment or so, release my clit to have a free hand to push down hard, flat-handed on my belly muscles, increasing the internal pressure on my pussy walls.

I think of my Master, bending me forward, taking me from behind, his cock testing and teasing my slit, gently seeking inside me, an inch only, against my entrance, making me twitch and moan and shudder, before ramming into me hard, grabbing me by the hair and pulling my head backwards, forcing me to arch my back and turning my moans into screams.

Rubbing hard at my inner walls, electric arousal sparks flames in my head. My thighs are wet and hot, and the bed is damp beneath me.

Again, I am moaning, trying to be quiet so as not to be heard through the thin walls to the next apartment. My pulse is racing, and I am sweltering under the sheets.

I throw off the covers and lie, naked and writhing, sleek with sweat, as I plunge my hand deep into my cunt. Again and again, I try to bring my Master within me, taking me with his cock, filling me hard until I can see nothing but him, feel nothing but him.

I want him in my pussy. I want him in my mouth. I want to feel him judder and spasm as he cums, spurting his load into me and on me.

I want him to orgasm over me, over my face and breasts and belly, into my aching pussy, into my mouth, letting me milk him, licking his cream from my lips and face.

Harder and harder I work myself, plunging my fingers in as deep as they will go, desperate for a substitute for my Master's body inside me. My hand is slick from fucking my own saturated pussy, my lips hot and swollen, pulsating with need and the desire for release.

It won't come. My orgasm just won't arise within me. I need more. Scanning my room, dimly lit from the streetlights, I spot a bottle of baby oil. It will do.

Grabbing the bottle, I slide it inside me. My aching cunt welcomes it, taking it in as I first test for fit, and then plunge it deep inside, fucking myself hard, again and again.

The bottle is slippery with oil and slick with my juices, but I ram it home, over and over. At some level, I am conscious that the headboard is clattering against the wall, but I don't care.

Now my orgasm builds, the tension mounting, blood pounding in my ears, my body arched rigidly, my thighs shuddering and trembling in my search for climax.

With an unquenchable heat, my orgasm takes me. My pussy sends pulsating spasms through my body. My thighs and stomach throb and clench in a rhythm that takes me completely, and I cry out, still working the bottle inside myself, making the ecstasy last as long as I can, drawing out the moment when my Master will leave me.

Pumping away at myself, I hold onto the crescendo as long as I can, before it becomes unbearable, and with a gasp, I whip the bottle out of my still spasming cunt and lie, gasping and panting, on the mattress.

As the climax passes and my breathing slows, there is banging on the wall. "Keep that fucking noise down!"

To hell with the neighbours. I'll be out of here soon.

The Story Continues in 'The Master's Fantasies'

Part Five

The Master's Fantasies

I do not see my Master for some days while he is out of town. When he does reappear at the office, on the occasions that I see him, he seems distracted and says little to me. I wonder if I have done something wrong, or worse, if he is growing tired of me.

Then, Francis, his personal assistant, buzzes me. "Beth, can you come up, please? He wants to see you."

"I'm on my way."

As I step out of the lift, Francis is sitting behind her desk outside the office, a thoughtful expression on her face. There are angry voices coming from behind the door to Richard's office.

Francis meets my eyes with raised eyebrows. "Hi, Beth. I'd take a seat if I were you. I don't know how long this is going to be."

The shouting continues. After a few more minutes, and with one voice becoming ever louder and angrier, Francis picks up the phone. "Frank? Yes? Can you send security up to the tenth floor, please? Yes, that's right. Now."

As she puts the phone down, the office door bangs open, and Mack Kane storms out, red-faced and furious. Slamming the door closed, he sees me and takes a step towards me, murder in his eyes. "Don't think I don't know it was you, you little bitch..."

I have no idea what he is talking about, and involuntarily I sit back in my chair as Mack steps closer to me, one hand raised.

Thankfully, the lift doors swish open and out step two blue-uniformed security guards. Mack sees them and backs off. At the same moment, Richard comes out of his office, looking stern but calm. "Francis, can you call Security, please... Ah, already here, I see. Thank you, Francis. Ben, Alan, can you please accompany Mr Kane to the exit. He will not be needing his security badge any longer. And he is not to be readmitted without my express permission."

He turns back to Francis. "Francis, please clear Mr Kane's desk and forward any personal effects to his home address."

Mack is almost purple with fury and turns to me, jabbing a finger in my direction with a clear threat in his eyes. "You bitch. You haven't heard the last of this..."

I am completely baffled. "I'm sorry, but I don't underst..."

Richard interrupts. "Are you threatening a member of my staff, Mr Kane? Should we call the police?"

Mack falls silent, but his face is still mottled red with fury. Stiffly, he turns and heads for the lift, accompanied by the security guards. As the doors swish closed behind them, Richard turns to Francis. "Make sure he's out of the building and that all the reception staff have clear instructions that he's not to be permitted back in. Then, get onto IT, and have his security codes and passwords changed immediately."

Francis nods. "Yes, Mr Haswell."

He takes a deep breath and stares up at the ceiling for a moment. Exhaling, he says, "Francis, a pot of coffee, please, as soon as you get the chance. Elizabeth, in here if you would. You deserve an explanation."

I follow him into the office, and he waves me to the settee.

"Elizabeth, I'm sorry. This wasn't your fault. When you brought me that file of *inconsistencies* that you said you didn't understand, you were quite correct. Those inconsistencies were not your misunderstanding of the procurement system. As I read through, and then when I investigated more deeply, it was quickly clear that what appeared to you to be the case, in fact, *was* the case. Someone was, in effect, having the same goods and services charged for twice, and sometimes more than twice. It would have been discovered at some point with a physical inventory count, but that could have been months away, and in the meantime, you have saved the company a great deal of money."

Francis enters with the coffee, deposits the tray, and leaves again. Richard pours two cups, and I sip at mine, a bit lost for words.

He leans forward and takes my hand. "Elizabeth, I can't tell you how grateful I am for your quick wits and your eye for detail. A lot of people would have, if they had spotted the problem at all, passed over the mystery and moved on. You struggled with it and came to me with your dilemma." He laughs. "It goes without saying that if you encounter any more such *inconsistencies,* I want you to come straight to me with them again."

I ponder the implications. "What will happen to him? Will you call the police?"

Richard shrugs. "I don't think so. It would be hard to prove that it was Mack. When I confronted him, he didn't deny it. However, I caught him out, unexpectedly, today. No doubt if the police came in, he would have his answers ready, and in the meantime, the company's shares would be falling. No, he's out, and he won't be coming back. And he'll not find it easy to get another job. You on the other hand..."

"What made him think it was me?"

"I didn't tell him that it was you, Elizabeth, but he knew which files you'd been looking at, and which projects you'd focused on. It didn't take him long to work it out when I started asking him specific questions."

I am really worried now. "He looked really mad. I thought he was going to hit me, but then the security guards arrived."

Richard pauses. "Is that right? Just like him to blame someone else for his situation." He rubs his chin. "Hmm... Just in case, I think we'll get you out of that old apartment of yours, *now.* Get you to a new address. Would you mind that?"

"Well, no, but I was going to move at the end of the month when I could make the deposit for the rent."

"I want you out of there before then. Where is the new apartment you have in mind?"

"It's in the Crown Towers development, you know, one of those new ones they've just built."

He smiles. "Yes, I know them. C'mon, let's go see." He buzzes the intercom. "Francis, can you call a car, please? We're going to be out for a couple of hours."

*****

In the privacy of the back of the car, I finally say, "I thought I had done something to upset you."

My Master looks startled. "Why would you think that?"

"Well, you dropped me off at my old flat last week and then I didn't see you again, or barely. And when I did see you, you didn't speak. I..." I falter. Am I safe to say this? "I... I missed you."

"I'm sorry about that, Elizabeth. I have to say that I also missed our, er... adventures together." He grins and wiggles his eyebrows at me. "Don't worry, I won't neglect you. I don't want you wandering off, looking for pastures anew."

"Oh, I won't do that. We have a deal, don't we? Anyway, I um... I sorted myself out," I confess, blushing crimson upon realising what I have just blurted out.

A rainbow of expressions crosses my Master's face - surprise, shock, and then, a sunrise of sensual pleasure. He tilts his head, and then taking my hand, he presses it against his groin, moving my hand in his, over him, showing me what is required of me. Through the fabric of his trousers, I feel his cock stirring to life.

He leans closer to me, his voice low and breathy by my ear. "So, you missed me, and you fucked yourself instead?"

"Yes, I did."

"Yes, what?" He presses my hand against his growing erection.

"Yes, Master. I fucked myself thinking about you."

"And?"

"I wanted you there, inside me. But you weren't there, so instead, I lay naked on my bed and got myself off."

"How? What did you do, Elizabeth? Tell me, in detail. I want to know."

I am unused to this and am not quite sure what to say, so I hesitate.

"Elizabeth, I have given you an instruction. I want you to tell me, detail by detail, how you fucked yourself."

"I spread my legs and I played with my clit." As I say this, my Master's cock jumps under my hand. I feel it straining for escape. As well as I can through his clothes, I work him with my fingers.

Ross's voice comes over the car intercom, "Sorry, Mr Haswell, we're stuck in a traffic jam. Might take a bit longer to get there."

I see my Master take a breath for voice control. He succeeds, and sounding very casual, replies, "That's fine, Ross. There's no hurry." Then he presses my hand down hard again.

Seeking permission in his eyes, I unzip and release my Master's now throbbing erection. "I'd have you down hard on that, sucking me off," he says. "But I want to hear what you have to say."

"I played with my clit," I repeat. "I rubbed myself and tweaked and flicked. And all the time, I was thinking of you, with your mouth around me, lapping at me and making me wet." With the tips of my fingers, I work the head of his penis, licking my fingers to make it as good as I can for him.

"I made myself really wet. I was ready for you, and I wanted you. I wanted you to lick me out, and then fuck me brainless." I feel that my fingers are not slippery enough. My Master's cock deserves better than this, so for a moment, I bend over, taking him in my mouth, licking and moistening the tender skin, but at the same time, I continue to slide my fingers up and down his length. My own panties are moistening.

"I used my hand and finger fucked myself," I continue. "But you weren't there. I was ready to be fucked properly. I wanted to feel you all the way inside me, balls-deep, but you weren't there. I would have used a vibe, but I didn't have one, so I had to find something else instead."

My Master is now leaking down my hand. As I hand fuck him, it is slippery and delicious, and I am becoming uncomfortable in my now soaking panties.

"What did you use? What did you bring yourself off with?"

"I found a bottle. It wasn't right, but it was good enough. I slid it inside me, and then I fucked my cunt, hard. I wanted you to fuck me, but instead, I used a bottle to fuck myself..."

Ross's voice comes over the intercom again. "We're clear, Mr Haswell. We'll be there in a couple of minutes."

Richard's eyes roll skyward. "Fuck!" he mutters.

I lean over him and lick him clean and dry, enjoying the taste of him and letting him see me lick my own lips clean. With a little difficulty, I tuck him away, and he pulls his jacket closed to cover his still overly obvious bulge.

*****

As we enter the lobby of the apartment block, the concierge does not at first even look up. "Yes?" he says. "What is it?" He is eating a sandwich, and casually brushes egg crumbs from his face onto his shirt.

I start to speak. "Hello. My name is Elizabeth Kimberley..."

Richard interrupts. "Is this how a member of my staff meets and greets members of the public?"

The concierge looks up sharply at him and then blenches. "Oh! Mr Haswell." He stands up hastily, struggling slightly to push his chair back as he does so. Then he plasters on an obsequious smile. "Sorry, Mr Haswell. I didn't know we were expecting you."

Richard leans forward over the desk, eyeballing the man. "You shouldn't need to be expecting the boss to show up to show common courtesy to a visitor to the building. That is your job. Do we understand each other?"

"Yes, sir."

"Get me the keys for 47A."

"Yes, sir." The concierge disappears into a back room for a moment, then reappears, jingling keys. "Here you are, sir."

"Thank you," Richard says. "And get a clean shirt on if you expect to be still working here next week."

We take the lift to the fourth floor. "I didn't know you owned this building too," I say.

He smiles and shrugs. "Handy, isn't it? And no one will disturb us." His smile turns to a wicked grin.

On the fourth floor, he unlocks the door and gestures me inside. As soon as the door is closed behind us, my Master grabs me by the arm and pushes me back against a wall. "Now, madam, you were explaining to me how you handle yourself alone." One hand grabs me by the wrists, gathering them and raising my arms above my head, pinning me to the wall. The other hand heads south, and not too gently, pulls up the edge of my skirt, questing up my thighs, past my panties, to between my legs. There is nothing restrained about his actions. My Master is ready now. His finger reaches in and up, straight inside me. I hear his grunt of satisfaction to find me already dripping for him.

With his face close to mine, he says, "Now, if you please, continue with your tale."

"I screwed myself with a bottle... hard."

His fingers plunge into me, and I yelp. "Like this?"

"Yes. Oh, God, *yes.*"

He stabs into me again, spreading his fingers as he goes, thumb outside, pressed on my clit, and I start to whimper in arousal. "You like that?"

I am breathless and gasping. "Yes... Yes." His thumb is rubbing my clit and I need to cum.

"You want more?"

"Yes. Please, yes."

"Yes, what?"

"Yes, Master, please fuck me. Please let me cum."

He leans even closer, whispering into my ear. "I'll forgive you this time because you didn't know. But in the future, you are only allowed to fuck yourself if you have asked my permission first. And afterwards, I expect a report, in detail, of what you did to yourself, for what is supposed to be a substitute for my fucking you properly. Do we understand each other?"

"Yes, Master, I think so." His fingers freeze. I am on the edge of an orgasm, brinking the precipice, and shaking with anticipation. I need to cum.

"The correct reply is, *Yes, Master*."

"Yes, Master. Please, Master. Please, let me cum."

"That's better." With his hand still inside me, fingers working my G-spot, he drops to his knees, splays my pussy lips with the other hand and wraps his tongue around my clit, flicking and tasting me.

Instantly, I orgasm, my pleasure pulsing electrically through me as I moan, gushing hot over my Master's fingers. "Spread your ankles," he commands and through a euphoric haze, I obey, trembling uncontrollably as my Master licks my thighs, clit, and pussy clean. My hips bucking, I want to give at the knees and let my weight slide to the floor, but he still has several fingers inside me. I can't take any more. "Oh, God! Stop, please stop. Please stop."

My Master sits back on his haunches, looking pleased with himself. "If that's the result of leaving you for a few days, perhaps I'll keep you waiting more often," he comments and then stands, holding out a hand for me. "And if I may suggest, in the future, keep some fresh underwear in your bag. I find that I want to make you drip." Speechlessly, I nod.

"And now to business. Shall we take a look at this apartment of yours?"

The apartment has one bedroom, with a nice open-plan lounge and kitchen area, a tidy little bathroom, and a lovely view over the park.

The area is good, and the apartment is brand new. Everything sparkles, unlike my old, dismal flat with its peeling paint and smell of dampness. I am so pleased to think that I will soon be living here.

Richard looks around quickly, seeming unimpressed. "It's very small," he comments.

"Yes, it is, but it's big enough for just me. And the area is so much nicer than my old place."

"What if you want friends to stay? Or your parents perhaps? And where can you work? There's no real place for a desk, or bookshelves, unless you have them in your lounge."

"It's fine. You can't have everything at once, and I can afford this now, which I certainly couldn't before."

Richard purses his lips. "Get your stuff from your old place. I'll send Ross to help you out. There's no reason for you to be in there any longer, and I'd rather not risk your being there, just in case Mack Kane knows where you lived."

A shudder goes down my spine. Mack had looked mad as hell with me, but surely he wouldn't be dangerous? Would he?

I nod and agree.

*****

Ross drops Richard back at the office, then helps me pack my small number of possessions into the car - a few clothes and personal items, my steam-driven laptop, and my books. None of the furniture is mine, and I wouldn't want it in my lovely new apartment anyway. When we return to the apartment block, with Ross staggering slightly under the weight of a cardboard box full of books, the concierge gives me a key. I notice that he is wearing a fresh shirt and is now sitting upright and alert at his desk.

"You've given me the wrong one," I say. "This is for 127A. Mine is 47A."

"That's the one Mr Haswell said I was to give you."

"Oh. Right." Puzzled, I take the lift to the twelfth floor, Ross following me.

The twelfth-floor apartment is amazing. High above the city, the gorgeous park view is below, but now the view opens far over buildings old and new, across the river, and out to the hills beyond. There are three bedrooms, a huge lounge and dining area overlooking those stunning vistas in three directions, and a bathroom to die for with all polished glass and chrome fittings as well as a Jacuzzi.

I am torn between a broad grin and embarrassment.

"Where do you want this?" asks Ross, still weighed down under his load.

"Umm... I'm not sure. Anywhere, Ross. Just put it down." I don't know quite what to do next. "I can't stay here. I can't possibly afford it."

Ross looks at me with a slightly pitying expression. "You're working for Mr Haswell?"

"Er, yes..."

"So, he pays your wages? He knows how much you earn?"

"Yes."

"And he's your landlord, so he sets the rent..."

"Err... yes..."

"And he told the concierge to give you this key?"

"Yes."

"So this is the apartment you're getting. And you can afford it. Now, where do you want this stuff?"

He's right, of course. What else can I say? I look around my new glorious apartment. Where to put things?

"Just put them down anywhere, Ross." I need to decide how to lay things out, and it's not as though there is any furniture yet.

I spend the rest of the day arranging my things as best I can with no furniture. I am just deciding that I should go out to shop for a bed, a table and chairs, and some other essentials when the door intercom buzzes. "Yes?"

"Hello, Elizabeth. It's me, Richard."

He's here!

"Oh, come on up. It's wonderful in here!"

A couple of minutes later, my Master enters then drops the latch on the apartment door. "I don't want to be interrupted right now." He smiles.

I start to speak. "I want to say thank you..."

He puts a finger to my lips. "You're welcome. But you can show me your thankfulness in a better fashion. Now where...?" He glances around the lounge and then walks to the kitchen counter. "Come here, Elizabeth."

I stand obediently before him as he tilts up my chin to kiss me on the mouth, then he gradually pushes me backwards towards the counter.

"Take your skirt and panties off."

Simply hearing him say those words excites me, and I feel that inner warmth rising again. I unzip my skirt, letting it slide down to my feet before stepping out of it and kicking it to one side. I then slip down my already noticeably damp panties. Pretty and black though they are, they are not needed. My stockings are enough.

As I stand up straight again, my Master is unbuttoning my blouse, sliding his hands inside, and then slipping it off my shoulders to also drop, discarded, to the floor. Next, he unhooks my bra, leaving me in only my black stockings.

For a moment he stands back, just looking at me, then he unclips my hair and pulls it tumbling down over my shoulders, a tumbling red torrent to match the fox at my loins.

"Undress me, Elizabeth."

I slip each shirt button slowly free, and then his cuffs, kissing the taut flat muscles of his abdomen as I do so. His bronzed skin contrasts sharply against the white linen of his shirt before it too falls to the floor. Unbuckling his belt and unzipping him, I am growing steadily wetter as I feel his already bulging erection. As I slide down his clothes, his hands push me down from the shoulders into a kneeling position, then, gripping my hair, he pulls my face towards him, as his other hand guides his penis into my mouth.

I lick off the twinkling droplet from the tip, loving the salty, sweet taste of his pre-cum. As my tongue and lips wrap around the head, his shaft twitches under me, and I revel in the odd feeling of power it gives me to obey this man, my Master, to do his bidding in everything.

With my mouth filled, I glance upwards to see him standing straight, head up and back, hands clasped behind his head. "Pay attention to what you are doing, Elizabeth," he says, and compliantly, I suck and lick his cock, feeling it pulse as I trail the tip of my tongue around the rim of the head, first flicking quickly, then making long sweeping strokes of my tongue, from the base of his shaft, full-length to the crown, savouring his trickling juices as his lust rises.

I hear him take a gasp above me. "You're so good at that, Elizabeth, but in a minute, you are going to stand, and I'm going to fuck you senseless."

At his words, I flood and gasp, feeling wet heat dribble down inside my thighs. He chuckles as he hears me. "You like that idea then?" Suddenly he bends, grasping me by the waist and lifts me, depositing my naked ass on the kitchen counter. "Spread 'em," he says, forcing my knees apart as he does so, and making me lean back to support myself. "Lie down," he says, pushing me, flat-handed, back down onto the marble surface, then pulling me forward at the hips until his cock kisses into my pussy.

He thrusts for a moment, then stops. "Not wet enough yet, I think."

I am not sure what he means by this, as it seems to me that I am already swollen and slippery for him, but he drops down and plants his mouth squarely over my pussy, thrusting in with his tongue, twisting and probing, drinking my juices. Involuntarily, I heave and gulp, arching my back to raise my hips to him, locking my ankles behind his head to open myself fully to my Master.

"Lie still," he says. "I have not given you permission to move."

I try to obey, but as his lips purse over my clit, I cannot help myself; I groan and writhe at the exquisite fire stabbing up through my core. My Master's teeth nibble gently at my bud, then his tongue circles it, flicking and manipulating it until my pussy juices gush over his face. He licks deep, over my pussy lips, trailing through my cunt, lingering deliciously as he drinks from me.

"Wet enough now, I think," he says as he rises to his feet.

Standing, my Master's erection is huge. He probes with the tip at my entrance, once, twice, thrice, as my pussy twitches and jumps in response, then thrusts hard, headlong deep inside me, stopping only as he strikes my inner walls. I scream in response, my cunt throbbing to his rhythm as I try to tighten my pussy and belly muscles around him. I can barely think as he plunges into me, again and again, but I know that I want him there and that I want him to take the greatest pleasure in me.

He pounds away inside me, no gentleness, and demanding a response. Lying flat-backed on the stone surface, there is little I can do beyond scream, it rises unbidden from my depths, a deep, primal reply to the earthquake of the flesh I am experiencing at my Master's bidding. My hips try to gyrate in time to his thrusting, but with no give to the stone surface, I cannot really move at all, only quiver below him as he plunges inside me, again and again, harder and harder.

I feel the stone slab slick under me, and I begin to slide over the smooth surface. My Master seizes me at the hips, holding me steady, as he continues his pounding inside me, balls-deep and then out completely to his full length, in and then out again. Breathing is difficult as I pant uncontrollably between screams, my heart pounding and my pulse racing.

I feel the rise of my orgasm within me, the tension building and my belly muscles clenching as it builds. Convulsing in a paroxysm of ecstatic joy, I try to lean up to embrace the sensation, but my Master's hand, flat between my breasts, pushes me down on my back again, holding me pinned as my climax overtakes me.

I am unconscious of anything but the release, as my pulsating cunt sends violent waves of pleasure through my stomach and thighs. I do not know if I scream, gasp, or cry, only that I am lying helplessly writhing, speared by my Master as he gazes down on me, cumming at his command.

Sated and exhausted, I lie there, my panting subsiding, as my Master locks eyes with me. "Don't move," he says. "You haven't finished."

He draws level with my face, and once again, seizes hold of my hair, pulling up my face. "Open wide."

I open my mouth and he pushes inside. "Finish me off," he commands. "I want to see you swallowing my cum."

"May I use my hands as well?"

"Yes, you can play with my balls while you lick me clean, then suck me off."

One-handedly, I massage his scrotum, tight and crinkled, palming at the harder kernels within. With the other, I support his huge erect penis as I lick away my own juices and his.

With one hand kneading his balls and the base of his erection, caressing and stroking, fondling and rubbing, I feel the growing throb and cadence of his rising climax. His own hips start to quiver, and then, as I feel he is going to spurt into my mouth, I slide the tip of my tongue into the slit of his penis, tickling, probing, and stimulating at this, his most sensitive moment.

In response, he exhales with a gasp, leaning forward and pulling me in deeper by my hair. He spurts into my mouth in a creamy cascade, and then pulling my mouth free of him, he finishes his climax over my face, his stream surging over my eyes and lips, dripping down into my hair. As he shoots his cum over me, I lick and suck where I can, taking what he gives as he rubs his cock and balls and cum over my face.

Finally, with a heave, he pulls free of me and stands, breathing deeply, arms akimbo.

After a moment he looks up again. "Elizabeth, you are *good.* You are so good." And he leans over, kissing me deeply on the mouth and then my breasts. "Come on, let me help you down." He picks me up from the marble, placing me carefully on my own two feet.

I wobble a little, a bit unsteady after the internal pounding he just gave my still swollen pussy and clit.

"A shower, I think," he says. "Let's check out your new bathroom."

The shower stall is roomy enough for two, and with the hot water cascading over us both, my Master soaps and then sponges me down. He gives special attention to my breasts and between my legs, sucking my nipples as he reaches between my thighs. "Don't worry," he comments. "I don't expect you to perform again quite this soon. But I enjoy the feel of your body."

Afterwards, we sit on the carpet in my still unfurnished apartment, looking out over the city and the river.

"How much furniture do you have?" he asks.

"None really. It all belonged to the landlord in my old flat. It's not a problem. I'll go and get some over the next few days." Then I try to collect my thoughts. "Thank you. The other flat was nice, but this is gorgeous."

"Yes, the other was all right, but this one is better. You have the space for guests and for an office or study here. Speaking of which, we have plenty of spare furniture in the basement back at the office, desks, bookshelves, that kind of thing. Pick out what you want and I'll get it sent over for you. It will do for you until you have had a chance to choose what you want and make the place your own."

I don't know what to say, so I settle for, "Thank you."

He smiles and kisses the top of my head. "You're welcome, Elizabeth. But we made a deal. You are keeping your end of it, and I am keeping mine."

Inside my heart sinks. Everything he says is true, but I don't want it to be a contract. I am falling in love with my Master.

The Story Continues in 'The Master's Obsession'

Part Six
The Master's Obsession

I am just putting the finishing touches to the bedroom in my beautiful new apartment when the door buzzes.

"Hello, Elizabeth. It's Richard."

With a thrill, I rush to the intercom. "Hi! Come straight up. The door's open."

When my Master arrives, he is carrying red roses and a briefcase. I recall that the very first time I saw him, he was carrying this same briefcase and he also had a bunch of red roses. He had a date, but the date had stood him up.

I wonder what he has in the case. The last time it was a spreader bar and a vibrating egg, both of which he tried out on me, giving me one of the most electrifying experiences of my life. I am becoming excited in anticipation. What is he planning?

He hands me the roses with a smile. "I hope you like them?"

"Oh, yes, Master, they're lovely. I'll put them in water."

He flops down onto the settee. "So, Elizabeth, we're celebrating your new home," he says, his gorgeous smile crinkling around his eyes.

I am so stirred by all this, my new life, my new apartment, and my Master, who I admit to myself, I am falling in love with.

"How would you like to celebrate?" he asks.

My eyes slide across to the briefcase. "I think you might already have ideas about that, Master."

He laughs. "Oh, yes, I do, lots of ideas, always. But this is *your* celebration, Elizabeth. And I want to thank you for what you have done, and are doing, for me. Tonight, you can tell me what you would like."

"I'd like..." my voice trails away.

Can I ask this?

He tilts his head in that now familiar gesture. "Yes?"

"I'd like..." I cannot speak, a lump is in my throat and tears begin to well up inside me.

He stands, concern on his face, taking me by the shoulders and holding me tightly to him. "Elizabeth, what's the matter? I want you to be happy. I thought you *were* happy. How have I upset you?"

"Oh, I *am* happy. I am. But..."

He holds me away from him now by the shoulders, squaring up to my face and holding my gaze. "Elizabeth, you have to tell me what's wrong. How can I make things right for you, if I don't understand your problem?"

"I... I want you to make love to me," I blurt out then fall silent, wondering if I have just ruined everything. My Master and I have a contract - a no-strings contract.

My Master looks startled then laughs. "I thought you enjoyed our little games, Elizabeth? Was I wrong?"

"Oh, no, you're not wrong at all. I love our *games.* It's just that..."

My Master falls silent, looking around the room. Moving to stand by the window, he stares out, his back to me. "Are you falling in love with me, Elizabeth?"

I hold silent for a moment but then take my courage in my hands. "Yes, I am..." I hang my head. "Are you angry with me?"

He almost whirls around, grabbing me again by the shoulders. "How could I be angry that one of the most beautiful women I have ever known, the most intelligent, and certainly the sexiest, is falling in love with me?"

Suddenly, he crushes his mouth onto mine, almost bruising my lips in his fervor, crushing me in his embrace. I respond hungrily, leaning into the kiss, exploding inside as he scoops me up, carries me through to the bedroom and, unceremoniously, dumps me onto the bed.

"I'll show you how a man makes love to a fucking star like you, Elizabeth."

There is a sparkle in his eyes and his smile is like sunshine as he sits beside me, enfolding me in his arms, his kiss deepening by the moment. I am totally unprepared by the sheer scale of my physical response to this. I am afire. In my head, skies are blue, the sun is bright, and birds are singing.

With my Master sucking and nibbling at my bottom lip, my heart begins to pound as I heat within, a familiar moistness between my legs. He trails kisses down my neck, and then struggling briefly with the buttons of my blouse, he unhooks my bra with one hand, cupping a breast with the other to suckle. As he sucks and nips at my puckering nipple, I am working at his shirt. I want his naked skin and the smell of his maleness all over me.

Sitting up, he helps me with the shirt, simply pulling it up over his head before discarding it onto the floor, and then shucks off his trousers and shoes. His now naked body, bronzed, lean muscled, and lightly haired, smells deliciously musky. I have never been certain if this is his personal scent or some aftershave that he uses, but it is deliciously *his* scent, and right now, it feels like my personal property.

He slides fingers behind my skirt to unzip it and slip it off me. Wearing nothing but white lacy panties, I lie back for him, arching my stomach and hips up to him as he plants kisses between my breasts, down my belly, and beyond.

His fingers slip between my legs, pausing briefly to ply my thighs apart, his fingers stroking the delicate inner skin. I am already wet as his fingers part my labia, exploring my swelling nub, sliding back the hood to reveal the sensitive heart within.

He is gentle and tender, working to arouse, and succeeding, and I curve and strain to meet him, my ardour becoming hard to control.

"Please, Master. I want you inside me."

"Easily done," he says, smiling as he repositions himself.

I watch his magnificent erection, which is quivering slightly against the flat of his abdomen. Lowering himself onto me, he pauses momentarily, allowing me to stroke his length and to kiss away the trembling droplet at the tip. Licking his salty-sweet honey from my lips, I draw him towards me as he lies full-length atop me, the tip of his cock brushing my pussy. He holds himself there, not entering, but teasing and arousing, knowing well that I want him to plunge inside me. Pressing lightly in, he then withdraws, instead kissing me, open-mouthed, with one hand kneading one of my breasts and tweaking the nipple.

"Oh, God, Master! Please get inside me. I want you inside me."

He whispers into my ear, "All in good time. Women don't always cum from penetration only. I want to make sure that you do." And he continues his plying and rolling of first one nipple, then the other.

I am wild with desire. Every time his cock leans in towards me, I rock my hips towards him, trying to swallow him into my depths, but always he withdraws, leaving me shaking with anticipation. I am yearning to have him fill me, aching to have his length fill my pussy. My juices are flowing freely, and the sheets are damp below me. Sweat glistens on my chest, my skin slick and shiny in the half-light.

Finally, when I think I might pass out if he makes me wait any longer, he first probes my pussy, then smoothly sheathes himself inside me. I gasp and cry out, my head flinging back and then forward, my eyes closing instinctively. I barely know what to do with myself from the ecstasy I am feeling from within.

In he slides and out, in and out; neither hard nor gentle, but rather steady and even, and smooth as silk, with a heartbeat rhythm. My own heartbeat is wild, my pulse banging wildly at my temples with the gliding thrust of my Master filling my pussy, making me moan and pant.

Opening my eyes, my Master is gazing down watching my face as he works me. His eyes are deep and intense. I could drown in them. His teeth lightly gritted, I see a sheen of perspiration as he draws me to my climax.

It begins, rising from my core, rippling out through the muscles of my belly and thighs. As I convulse inside, my Master responds by thrusting hard, in his pulse-beat rhythm, my cunt squeezing his cock as I erupt into a mind-blowing orgasm.

Through my physical rapture, I am conscious of his arms encircling me as I cum, and his kisses on my neck and breasts. Gliding down once more from the heights of passion, I feel warm breath by my face and fingers running through my hair.

My Master does not cease his thrusting. Kissing me briefly on the lips, he raises himself over me as he thrusts, looking down on me as he builds to his own climax. And now, I stroke his face, reaching up to caress his beautiful features as I move with his rhythm, trying to gift him what he just gifted me. With my pussy, I relax as he glides in, squeeze as he pulls out, trying to make it good for him. His sweat drips onto my breasts, trickling over my hot damp skin, anointing me with his scent.

With a gasp, his eyes shut tightly, and he shudders into his orgasm, groaning as his hips buck, his cock pressing deeply inside me. With his chest heaving, he collapses on top of me and simply lies there as I comb his damp hair with my fingers, kissing the side of his face.

For a long minute, we lie there, unmoving, my mind full of glory. My Master has not said that he loves me, but he is not angry with me.

Perhaps I can yet hope for more than a contract...

"Master?"

He pulls himself up onto an elbow, once more looking down on me. His smile is like sweet honey to me. "Yes, Elizabeth?"

"What just happened?"

"What happened?" he laughs. "What happened is that I, as requested by a beautiful girl who says she is falling in love with me, made love to her. That is what you wanted, isn't it?"

Dumbly, I nod.

His face turns serious. He takes my chin in his hand, looking me straight in the eyes. "Elizabeth, don't misunderstand. I can't claim that I love you. I am very fond of you, and I really, *really* lust for you. I hope that is enough for you, for now at least?"

Again, I nod. Yes, it is enough for me...

...for now.

"Good!" He rises and stretches. "And now, I think, let's have that celebration for your new home. Dinner out, I think, yes?"

"Mmm. Yes, lovely."

*****

The following day, while walking home from the office, I decide to do a little window-shopping; I still need a few things to furnish my apartment. I am staring through the shop window of one of the plusher furniture stores when, in the reflection, I see behind me a figure I recognise - Mack Kane, ex-head of the procurement department. He is glaring at me from across the street. I always found him unappealing, something about him making my skin crawl, but now he looks positively toxic.

As I spin to face him, he turns his back, walking quickly from view around a corner. A shudder runs through me. Is it a coincidence? Or am I being followed by this man who lost his highly paid job as a result of my discovery of his theft from the company?

Perhaps my imagination is running riot. Nonetheless, I go inside the store to lose myself in the crowds. I exit a few minutes later through a different door. If Mack is following me, I do not want him to know where I live. Should I mention this to Richard?

No, I decide, not without being a bit more certain of what is happening. For now, I will simply be alert. If Mack is following me, I will soon find out.

Over the next few days, I do not see him again and I conclude that I have an over-vivid imagination. No doubt he just happened to be in that street. Putting it from my mind, I focus on my work, my training, and my wonderful Master.

Francis buzzes me. "Hi, Beth. Can you come up, please? Mr Haswell would like a word."

Up on the tenth floor, my Master makes me welcome in his office. "Hello, Elizabeth. I just wanted a quick chat. Coffee?"

"Thanks, yes, I'd love one."

He rings through a request to Francis then returns his attention to me. "I have a meeting tomorrow. A very important meeting with potential clients who, if we can get the deal, will be worth a great deal of money to the company."

"Okay." I nod attentively.

What does this have to do with me?

"I would like you to sit in on the meeting."

Oh!

"You have already proved that you have an eye for detail with your work in the procurement section. It may have been an unpleasant little episode, but it saved the company a lot of money. Tomorrow, I want you to sit in as secretary to the meeting and take the minutes."

He leans forward. "Elizabeth, I want you to bring in that talent for detail again. Take notes of what is said - proposals, agreements, suggestions, whatever there is. However, I also want you to watch the people - body language, expressions. Do they seem comfortable with the discussion? Does anyone look unhappy with the agreement? That sort of thing." He takes my hand in his. "Are you with me on that? Happy with it?"

I nod. "Yes, it sounds fine to me. What...?"

I do not get to finish my question. At that moment, we hear raised voices in the outer office; Francis' and some other female voice I don't recognise. The office door slams open, almost bouncing back on its hinges, and a woman strides in, her face like fury. She should be rather attractive, beautiful even, with immaculate makeup, expensive designer clothes, and sleek dark hair. However, her enraged expression spoils her beauty.

Francis follows her in, gesturing apologetically at my Master.

The stranger snaps, "Richard! This *fucking* woman of yours tried to tell me I can't come in." Then, registering me, she halts mid-stride, raising one eyebrow.

My Master stands, not looking pleased. "Adele, it is Francis's job to ensure that I am not disturbed when I am in a meeting."

Her lip curls. "Yes, I can see what kind of meeting you are having. Who's this then? Your latest little trollop?"

My Master takes a deep breath, then speaks in measured tones, his voice tight with suppressed anger. "If it were any of your business, Adele, I might answer that. But it isn't. The last time we met, if you recall, you stood me up. At the time, I took it as an informal way of you finally saying goodbye. I still do. Now, please leave. Feel free to call me this evening, *if* you think we have something to discuss. Right now, I would like to return to my discussions here."

She stands frozen for a moment, her head back, and wearing that arrogant ugly lip curl, then turns her gaze to me. "I wouldn't hope for too much, dear." She spits the words. "You're not the first. You won't be the last." She spins and marches out, followed by Francis.

My Master waits a few seconds then follows them out. I hear him speaking. "Francis, check with reception that she's left the building, would you? Then cancel her entry codes. I don't want any repeat of this."

"I'm sorry, Mr Haswell. I tried to stop her bursting in like that, but she wouldn't have it. You know what she's like..."

"Yes, I remember well, *just* what she is like. Don't worry about it, Francis. It's not your fault. Just make sure that she can't simply march in like that again."

He comes back into the office and sits down next to me again. "My apologies, Elizabeth. That wasn't fair on you. It won't happen again."

"That's all right. It wasn't your fault. Was she... Were the two of you..." My tongue ties.

How do I ask this?

"Yes, we were... But not now, or ever again. The last time I saw her was the night you and I met, when you decided to take an impromptu shower in my bathroom if you recall..." He grins, and my tension subsides a little.

While it was happening, I did not have time to be upset by Adele's outburst. It was over too quickly, but now the meaning of her words is beginning to sink in. I am beginning to feel a little sick.

My Master sees this in my face. "Elizabeth, you mustn't be upset by this. I do not *want* you upset by this."

I nod and gulp but can think of nothing to say.

He grips me by my arm and tilts my face up, forcing me to look him in the eyes. "I know that you want more than I am offering, but I will make you no promises I do not believe I can keep. For now, you must accept that. But..." His grip on my arm tightens, almost hurting me. "*But...* she is part of my past. That night you and I first met, I was taking one last shot at making it work with her, God knows why."

He releases me, and standing, sweeps his hair back with both hands, staring at the ceiling. "Anyway, whatever the reason, I tried. You just got a taste of her personality. And she was never really any different, even when I thought there might be something real between us. The reality is that she is manipulative, scheming, and really not very pleasant to know. I was simply besotted with her physical beauty. Whereas you, Elizabeth..." His smile returns as he looks at me. "... You are as sweet as Spring, and I will do my best to honour every promise I make you, because I know that you will do the same. Are you all right, Elizabeth?"

Biting my lip, I reply, "Yes, I am. Thank you, Master."

"Good, let's get back to work, and then later perhaps, we should continue celebrating your new apartment, eh?"

"Oh, yes, Master." I laugh.

"You can wear that rather attractive green bodice you have. It goes with your hair beautifully."

"Yes, Master."

*****

But that evening, on my way home, I become aware of being shadowed again. Trying not to show that I know I am being followed, I pause again by shop windows, trying to pick out my stalker in the reflection, but he always slips out of sight before I spy him. Mack again?

Unnerved once more, I cut through the crowds to lose myself before continuing home. I decide that I must tell my Master what is happening.

*****

The green bodice my Master likes was chosen for him. I try to select clothes I think he will enjoy. Carefully I fit it into place, supporting my large breasts, but with the laces dangling free.

Matching side-laced panties and black lace stockings are, I think, all else that is needed. Possibly, I will not be wearing them for very long...

My Master strides into the apartment just as I finish preparing myself for him. Clearly, he is in the mood for action as, with no preliminaries, he pushes me flat back against the wall. "Stand there. I want to look at you." Then, moving back for a better view, he says, "Lift your chin. I want to see your face properly."

Obediently, I comply, tilting my face a little, to allow my Master to see my profile.

He seems pleased with the effect. "Do you have any champagne here?"

"Yes, Master. Shall I fetch it?"

"Yes, with glasses and ice."

When I return, he is seated on the settee, sprawling a little, arms raised, hands clasped behind his head. His eyes follow me as I pour the wine and offer him a glass.

"Just put it on the table for now then come here. Stand in front of me."

Again, I obey, placing myself before him, his face level with my hips.

"Closer. I want to be able to smell you."

I move closer, my panties now almost brushing his face. He leans forward, one hand caressing my hip and thigh as he inhales deeply. "You smell wonderful, Elizabeth, but then you always do." He leans back again onto the settee. "Now, play with yourself."

I hesitate, a little unsure of what he is asking.

"I said, play with yourself. Finger yourself. Play with your clit. Fuck yourself. I want to watch you arouse yourself. Then, when you're good and wet, I'm going to fuck you."

Sliding fingers down the front of my panties, I rub, weaving through red curls so that my Master can see the movement through the green silk. His head tilts and his eyes are dark, his pupils wide as he watches. I allow a few foxy hairs to escape the lace of the panties, rosy against the white of my thighs.

My Master is not exactly smiling, but his teeth show a little, white against his tan as I see his breathing deepening. "I don't think we need those, do we?" he says, and one-handed, he teases apart the side laces of the panties, discarding them.

"Unlace the top of your bodice. I want to see your breasts."

Slowly, I pull the laces of the bodice open, allowing my heavy breasts to swing free from their confinement.

"Now, closer. Then start fucking yourself again."

I stand close to him, as he leans farther back into the settee and says, "Closer. I want to see everything."

I try to move closer, but cannot as my knees chafe against the couch.

"Closer," he says. "Kneel up. Straddle me."

Kneeling up, my legs parted astride my Master, he supports me with his hands on my hips, steadying me. "Now," he commands. "Play with yourself. I want to see you dripping."

This will not be difficult. The act of opening myself, so close to my Master's face that I can feel the heat of his breath on my loins, is already arousing me and my pussy is moistly warm.

Slipping fingers between my legs, I start to play with my clit, pulling the hood back with one hand and rubbing it with the other. Working at my nub, it grows hard under my fingers. A couple of fingers in my pussy for a moment give me a little juice to lubricate myself, making my clit more slippery and easier to work.

"Put your hands on my shoulders. Support yourself," my Master demands.

Taking one hand from my hips, he parts my lips, leaning in close to suckle at me. His tongue lapping at my bud is electric, and I moan, struggling to remain still in my awkward position balanced over him.

"I did not give you permission to move," he says, withdrawing from me for a moment then returning to his work, nibbling at me, chewing lightly at my labia, and working my clit with his tongue.

My breath is shuddering now, and my balance is precarious.

"Take your hands from my shoulders. Support yourself against the back of the couch."

My Master slides down now directly under me, my pussy open for his inspection. Looking up, he peruses my folds like a gourmet, tasting and licking, flicking at my clit with his tongue, working circles around it, and nibbling with his teeth.

I am very wet now, my breath ragged and broken. Pussy juices trickle and my Master licks them away. He tongues my entrance, probing, first lightly, and then more deeply. His face presses close to me, drinking my depths as I judder and squirm, fighting the impulse to buck my hips. With my face flushing, sweat trickles down between my breasts.

Through my growing euphoria, I hear something - a buzz. A vibe? Where did he get it from? His pocket? I have no time to wonder as, abruptly, my Master pins me by one thigh, arm wrapped tightly around my leg. In the same moment, he applies the vibe to my clit, sending waves of electric stimulation shooting through me. I squeal in shock, convulsing reflexively as he circles my clit with the vibe, first probing into the root, then skimming the tip, now sensitized and swollen. Juices gush from my throbbing cunt, and an unbearable tension builds in waves, as my Master works mercilessly at my tender button.

My orgasm rises quickly, engulfing me in spasm after spasm of pleasure. At some level I am aware that my Master is no longer working my clit, but has buried himself in my pussy, drinking from me as I cum, his mouth locked over me, his tongue penetrating, prolonging my climax as I shudder and scream.

Barely does my orgasm subside when he pushes me away and down onto the floor. Standing, he towers over me, stripping off his shirt and pants. As they drop in a heap beside me, he says, "On your hands and knees, Elizabeth. Ass up. I want to see you."

Submissively, I obey, dropping down to rest on my elbows, my head well down so that my naked buttocks are presented for my Master.

"Good girl. Now stay there." He strides to his briefcase and extracts a red and black leather paddle. I recognise it; I bought it for him as a birthday present.

He walks around me, stroking me with the paddle, skimming my hair with it, sliding it over my spine. Lightly, he taps a bare buttock with it, and I quiver in anticipation.

"You like that, eh?" He taps the other buttock, harder this time, making me yelp. "Be quiet," he commands. "Tonight, I think I'm going to test your limits a little. You remember your safe word?"

"Yes, Master. *Redhead.*"

"Good. Let's see how far you want to ride..."

A tingle runs down my spine. I have barely come down from the waves of one orgasm, but already I feel my body's response to my Master. Biting my lip, nonetheless, my pussy juices flow, trickling down my thighs.

"I can see that, Elizabeth. I know you're enjoying this. Now... a question for you. I can either fuck you from behind or face-fuck you. Which is it to be?"

"I don't mind, Master. You choose."

With a *thwack!* that makes me gasp, the paddle slaps across my rear. "Wrong answer, Elizabeth. Now, do I shove my cock up your cunt or do I push it down your throat?"

My ass is smarting. "My mouth, Master. My mouth."

Thwack! The paddle lands again, but this time harder and I yelp.

"Your mouth? What about your mouth?"

"Shove your cock in my mouth, Master. Face-fuck me."

The paddle drops to the ground beside me, and this time instead, I feel my Master's hand slap across my butt, hard this time, really hard. I yell in pain, but my Master is not fooled because my throbbing pussy gushes.

"I still think you're enjoying this, Elizabeth." His hand rams hard inside me, three fingers pumping in and out. "Ask nicely. If you want me to face-fuck you, ask nicely and tell me what you want me to do."

"Please, Master. Let me suck you off. Let me make you cum."

"And then?" *Thwack!* The hand slaps this time, not my buttocks, but my aching and streaming cunt. This time it really hurts, and I almost rise, jolted off my elbows by the pain. But as I start to rise, my Master grabs me by the hair, pinning my head low again. "Did I tell you to move?"

Gasping, I say, "No, Master."

With his hand pressing my head to the carpet, my Master kneels between my splayed legs, forcing my knees a little farther apart with his and opening my pussy wider with his fingers. His erection presses against my smarting lips, then thrusts inwards.

I am slick and slippery. There is no resistance as he pumps into me, hard, meeting my inner walls. Although my elbows are still on the ground and my back arched to present my open pussy, he pulls my head back and up by my long red hair, making it difficult to breathe as I gasp and pant.

"Be quiet!" And still pumping me, he slaps my butt in time with his rhythm, first one side, then the other.

I am close to as much as I can stand. "Redhead!" I yell. "Redhead! Please, Master. No more."

Instantly he withdraws from me and stands. "On your knees, Elizabeth." And as I kneel up to him, he forces his finger between my lips. "Open!" he commands.

His cock is hugely erect and dripping with my juices as he presses into my mouth. As I wrap my lips and tongue around him, I know that it will not be long. Already I taste the honey salt of his pre-cum, and as I steady myself with one hand on his thigh, I feel the tension and the quiver of his build-up to climax.

I bind my lips tightly around my Master's shaft, feeling the strain and the pulse of his pre-climax building at the base as I massage his balls with my free hand. Slipping my tongue around the head and into the sensitive slit, I gag as suddenly, he thrusts deep, pinning me by my hair as he shudders and groans into climax, spurting into me.

I cough and splutter as his cum fills my mouth, catching me at the back of my throat. Deep in orgasm though he is, my Master feels that I am choking and pulls free, shooting instead over my face and into my hair.

As his climax ebbs, I look up to see him with his eyes tightly shut, his face still locked in a grimace.

Relaxing, he opens his eyes, looking down at my cum-spattered face. "You're beautiful, Elizabeth," he says. Then wiping his cum from my face, he adds, "A little disheveled, but beautiful."

He offers me a hand, helping me stand. I stagger, my sore bottom making me a little stiff.

"Are you all right, Elizabeth?"

"Yes, Master, I'm fine, really." In fact, I am better than fine. I feel wonderful.

I am not going to spoil the moment. I will tell my Master about Mack Kane tomorrow.

The Story Continues in 'The Master's Sin'

Part Seven
The Master's Sin

"So, what do you think?" asks my Master. "How did it go?"

We are sitting in his office, following a meeting with Alexander Thornton, Senior and Jaye Thornton, Junior.

My Master, Richard Haswell, is negotiating a real estate deal with them worth tens of millions. I have been acting as secretary at the meeting, taking the minutes. Also, I have been acting on instructions from my Master to be his eyes and ears; to gauge reactions, to *people-watch.*

What do I think?

I sip my coffee, choosing my words.

"I think that Thornton Senior wants the deal. He thinks that being associated with the Haswell Corporation will enhance his company's reputation and that he will be able to pass that legacy to his son. However, I also think that Thornton Junior believes the opposite; that their company will be swallowed whole by Haswell and lose its identity. It doesn't matter to him how attractive the deal is financially. He doesn't want his father's company to appear to be the junior partner."

My Master chews his bottom lip, staring up at the ceiling for a minute. "I think you're spot on with that, Elizabeth. Any suggestions on how to deal with it?"

Sipping my coffee, I ponder for a minute. "Well, the actual deal is all but agreed, isn't it? The legalities, the finances, the share split, and so on. Am I right on that? No one is saying that the deal discussed is unfair, or poor value?"

Nodding, "Ah-ha... I would say that's correct, yes."

"Well, in that case, it's about face-saving surely? Giving a perceived value to their input."

"Okay. So...?"

"Suppose that some of the more visible parts of the project were branded with their company name, or even better, *their* names. For example, there's a theatre complex planned as part of the development isn't there? It could be called something like the Alexander Thornton Arts Foundation perhaps? I don't think that would make any difference to you, would it?"

My Master snaps his fingers. "Perfect! You're right. It's all about Jaye Thornton's ego. And you are quite correct. I don't need my self-image boosting. We'll see if a little flattery will win their hearts *and* the deal."

*****

Later that evening, we are sitting in a beautiful restaurant; myself and my Master, with Alexander and Jaye Thornton. The surroundings are lovely, the staff excellent and the food is divine. However, the mood is tense.

Alexander Thornton is a man of perhaps sixty years old, silver-haired, twinkly-eyed and charming. His son, Jaye Thornton is a firecracker, quick-tempered, good-looking and eager to take offence. I wonder how serious his father is about passing his company on to this impetuous young man.

"So," begins my Master, addressing Thornton Senior. "What are your conclusions after our discussions this afternoon? It seems to me that our offer is acceptable. The project is viable and both our companies have skills to bring to the table."

Jaye jumps in before his father can speak. "No, it is *not* acceptable. Everything is set up so that *your* company sees all the benefits, receives the publicity. Everything. The Thornton Corporation..."

His father breaks in. "Now then, Jaye. Calm down. This can work for everyone. We just have to find the right way of doing it."

"I agree," says my Master. "In fact, Elizabeth has some thoughts on this very point..." He turns to me, gesturing, inviting me to speak.

Nervously, "Well, Mr Thornton..."

Smiling, "Alex, my dear..."

I nod acknowledgement of his courtesy. "Alex. Earlier today, you were talking about how you wanted to pass your company onto your son..." I nod to Jaye, trying to address them both. "... You were saying that you would like to retire and you were considering your legacy; how you would be remembered for all the work you have done to build up your company..."

Alex nods encouragingly.

"Well, I was thinking that, in the eyes of the world, company names don't mean much do they? But other things do. Things that are more visible to the man in the street. John Doe doesn't care about the name on the *Constructed By* billboard. But if, for example, the theatre complex were to be called something like *The Alexander Thornton Arts Foundation*, it would mean a lot more to him. The park area could be perhaps, *The Thornton Recreational Facility.*" I grind to a halt, feeling a bit of a fool.

However, Jaye's eyes have lit up. "That would be wonderful. Dad here would get the recognition he deserves for all his hard work, and the Thornton Corporation gets the prestige that it deserves."

My Master swings his gaze to Thornton Senior. "So, Alex. What do you think?"

"I think we have a deal, Richard." He stands, hand offered.

My Master shakes hands with both Thorntons. "I'll get the lawyers on to writing up a draft form of words tomorrow. We'll get something to you by Thursday for approval."

"Agreed. And I think a toast to celebrate our agreement." Alex holds up a champagne flute and we all clink glasses.

The remainder of the evening is spent in pleasant chit-chat.

Alexander says "So, what is your position in all this, Elizabeth? Obviously, you are part of the company, but do I take it that you and Richard are...?"

I am unsure how to answer this, not knowing what my Master has told people about me. However, he smoothly interrupts my confusion. "Yes, Alex. You're quite right. Elizabeth and I *do* enjoy more than a business relationship." He takes my hand and kisses it, his eyes soft as he gazes into mine.

As the conversation continues, light now, and cheerful, everyone smiling and relaxed, my Master's hand strays down onto my thigh, stroking me. I do not think he actually intends anything by it or is even really aware he is doing it, as he is engaged in conversation. However, I have waited for this moment. My skirt was carefully chosen to be flattering, but apparently demure. To the outside world, I must appear a princess. Caesar's wife must be above suspicion. However, the skirt is a wrap-over, falling easily aside with a little assistance.

I shift my position slightly, allowing the fabric of the skirt to slide away, giving my Master access to my stocking top and naked thigh, discreetly hidden by the white linen tablecloth.

This, he does notice, and for a brief second, his eyes slide sideways to mine while he continues speaking with the Thorntons. However, his hand continues its smoothing massage of my leg, gradually working further upwards and inwards. I admire the skill with which his hand is moving, but his upper arm, visible to the outside world, remains stationary. And his conversation with Alex and Jaye continues unbroken.

Suddenly I see the look of shock pass over his face. He coughs into his napkin to cover it. Alex looks concerned. "Are you alright, Richard? Have a glass of water."

My Master nods and goes through the motions of drinking the water, but his eyes meet mine with an unreadable expression. His questing hand has just discovered that I am wearing no panties.

"More water, Richard?" I ask, in a voice of concern, keeping all trace of laughter from my tone.

"Thank you, Elizabeth. Yes, I'm getting a little warm in here."

*****

Arriving at my Master's apartment, he opens the door and eye points-me in. "*You.* Inside."

Obediently I enter, sucking in my cheeks as I try not to smile.

Closing the door behind him, my Master grabs me, shoving me up against the wall. "*That* was very naughty, Elizabeth. Not wearing panties for an important meeting. Suppose you'd had to bend over?"

"Sorry Master. But I didn't have to bend over, and I was very careful. You would never have known about it unless your hand hadn't..."

"Answering back is also not the way to behave." His voice is stern, but his eyes are laughing as he lifts me bodily against the wall.

My God, but he's strong...

"Put your arms around my shoulders," he instructs as he lifts my skirt, pulling it to one side and exposing my nakedness underneath. I anchor my legs around his waist as he probes my pussy with a finger. "As I suspected, sopping wet already, Elizabeth. I'll have to do something about that." His trousers are noticeably bulging.

I am trying, unsuccessfully, not to giggle as, while I hang around my Master's shoulders and waist, he unbelts and unzips, releasing his cock, already standing hard and stiff. My giggles turn to squeals as, with no ceremony, he pushes inside me, gently once or twice, opening me up, then *hard*, ramming home.

Thrusting into me he says "You needn't think you're going to get your own way this easily, Elizabeth. You're not allowed to cum yet.

This is just to give me a bit of relief before I give you the spanking you deserve. I had to sit through the rest of the evening with my cock twitching below the tablecloth. *You* are only going to come when that naked bottom of yours is bright red."

I am already thoroughly aroused. They say that the best sex always starts in the head, and the anticipation of waiting for my Master to discover my *dishabille*, on top of the success of my suggestion regarding the Thorntons, has left me riding high. My pussy is wet and warm, and my Master's hard fucking is rapidly bringing me to climax. He realizes this and withdraws.

Putting me down he orders "Into the bedroom. Bend over the bed."

I do as I am told, folding myself over the foot of the bed, my butt raised. My skirt has dropped down to cover me up again but my Master does not bother to remove it, simply flipping it upwards to display my naked buttocks and my engorged lips and pussy. "This is going to hurt, Elizabeth. You can't behave like that without being punished."

"Sorry, Master."

"Sorry's not good enough. This is only going to stop when you beg me for it." He slaps a buttock, hard.

I yelp, reflexively trying to stand, but his hand is on my back and he pushes me down again, face pressed to the bed. "Did I give you permission to move?"

"No, Master."

"Exactly. No." He slaps again, the other butt cheek. "You don't move until and unless I give you permission." This time the slap is onto my flooding pussy. And then another in the same place. The sting is exquisitely painful and utterly delicious. I do not know whether to scream or moan.

"I think you're enjoying this way too much, Elizabeth. Stay there. Don't move."

My Master exits the room, leaving me panting and trembling. I really, *really* want my Master to fuck me to orgasm, but I know I will have to wait. He returns and I can hear him moving behind me. I risk a quick look to see what he is doing.

He has taken off his shirt and is barefoot, wearing only his black belted trousers. Tanned, lean and athletic, he looks like a god as he approaches me from behind, holding a riding crop. I catch my breath at the thought of what is coming.

Can I handle this?

He traces the inside of my thighs with the tip of the crop, probing into my pussy, caressing my pulsing clit. "Open your legs further."

Awkwardly, I spread my legs further, feeling fingers insert into my slit as I do so, spreading my lips, widening me. Pussy juices trickle down my thigh. "Turned on, Elizabeth? Nice and sensitive? Good. I want you sensitive." His tongue licks upwards from clit to cunt, sending fire through my core. I moan helplessly.

"Remember, Elizabeth. This stops when you beg me to stop. Tell me you understand."

"I understand, Master."

"What do you understand?"

"That you will stop only when I ask you to."

"That's right. But you will have to ask nicely and make it worth my while to stop. I'm going to enjoy this." And he brings the crop down on my naked ass.

This time I do scream. But my pussy gushes, betraying my body to the pain. My head tells me that this is too much, but my body wants more.

My Master strikes at me again with the crop, and again. "Well, Elizabeth? Do you need more punishment?"

I cannot speak, only gasping breathlessly as my body aches for fulfilment.

"Repeat after me," he says. "I will always wear my knickers in business meetings."

"I will..." *Gasp...* "... always wear my knickers in business meetings."

The crop comes down again and now I am really feeling that I can take no more. The tip taps on my clit. "And now, Elizabeth. What is it to be?" The crop-tip slaps lightly up on my clit.

"Please, Master. I can't... I can't..."

"What is to be Elizabeth?"

"Please, Master. No more. Please stop."

The crop flicks harder across my clit. Enough to hurt. "I told you. You have to ask properly."

"Please, Master. No more. I'll be good."

"Will you? Will you be good? And what do I get?"

"Let me suck you, Master. Let me suck you off."

"Hmm... It might be worth it. Will you swallow my cum? Lick me clean?"

"Yes, Master."

"Alright. I'll stop." I start to rise, but he pushes me down again. "I didn't tell you to move." The crop slaps against my knees. "Wider. And push your ass up."

Still trembling and panting, I obey my Master, stretching my legs as far apart as I can. The crop explores between, and the tip settles on my clit. At the same moment, I hear the buzz of a vibe as it is pushed deep inside me.

The vibe is on a high-powered rise-and-fall cycle, and my already liquid core responds. The crop flicks at my clit, no gentle caress this. My tender nub is being bludgeoned, jerked and jolted by the clumsy tool. Nonetheless, I am brinking, panting to climax, heart pounding and pulse racing. My hips jerk and buck, but my Master slaps hard at my ass again. "Keep still! How am I supposed to fuck you like this, if you keep moving?"

Poised on the edge of orgasm, the world dances around my pulsating bud. I am sore and bruised, my naked butt stings and I can feel the weals decorating my rear, but nonetheless, orgasm is about to take me...

My Master licks my pussy, a long, slow stroke, circling and probing. The vibe still works its magic inside, and the crop tip pounds at my bud. Tipping over the edge, I detonate into climax, screaming as I go. All but collapsing onto the bed, I feel my Master supporting me at the hips, stopping me from falling. Writhing and bucking, waves of pleasure pulse through my cunt, my belly and my thighs before subsiding, and I drop, spent, onto the mattress.

For a long minute I lie, quiescent, before my Master, standing over me, bare-chested, glistening with sweat and arms akimbo says, "You haven't finished yet."

I nod, speechless, and kneel before him. "May I unbelt you, Master?"

"You may."

Erection bulging through the fabric, I undo the black leather belt and unzip. As his trousers fall to the ground, I scent the sweet musky perfume of his arousal. His penis is beautiful to me, and I kiss the tip, working my tongue around the ridge, cupping his balls as I do so.

Hands behind his head, eyes closed, he stands tall over me as I work him, licking long, smooth strokes up the length of his shaft, lapping away the dewdrop on the tip, wrapping my lips tight around the head as I suck.

His breathing is deep, becoming laboured. Massaging the base of his erection, his pulse pounds against my fingers. He's close.

Taking him in my mouth as deeply as I can, I work him with my tongue and lips, his pre-cum increasing to a steady stream, and I savour the cream as it trickles down my throat.

His breath shudders and suddenly his hands clamp to the back of my head, fingers twisting into my hair, as he starts to thrust into me.

Fighting to control my gag reflex, I want to take all of him into me, but he is simply too large. Already my mouth is stretching to accommodate him, and as his climax builds he feels even larger. He moves my head in time with his rhythm; in-out, in-out, face-fucking me for his pleasure.

With a groan, he spurts, shooting his sweet cum into my mouth. I try to swallow, but he presses into me and I cannot. My mouth and throat fill, as he grinds and pulses into me, then with a gasp, releases me and withdraws.

Wiping dripping lips with the back of my hand, I swallow his gift, relishing the briny flavour, then lean in again to lick him clean. sliding my tongue up his erection, he allows me only a couple of strokes before he pulls back, laughing, "Enough, Elizabeth. Enough!" Leaning down, he kisses me full on the mouth.

Offering me a hand, he helps me to stand, giving me a light slap on the rump. "I think, Elizabeth, that with the clothing allowance you have, you can afford to have underwear for all occasions. In future, when we are out in public, you will *always* wear panties... Unless of course, *I* instruct otherwise."

"Yes, Master."

*****

The deal goes well. My Master is pleased. Signed, sealed and delivered, a copy of the contract papers lands on my desk. "I want you to be familiar with them, Elizabeth," he says. "You were instrumental in making the deal work. I want you involved with its progress. Take the time to know the details, the legal ins-and-outs."

Fair enough. I settle to read my way through a book's worth of small print, and quickly decide that 'legalese' is heavy reading. However, the gist of the agreement is simple enough. The Haswell Corporation and the Thorntons are setting up a holding company to act as a legal envelope for a huge redevelopment in a run-down part of the City. The project is huge, involving the building or renovation of a vast acreage to provide luxury apartments, affordable housing and all the facilities and amenities needed for a properly functioning community; shops, offices, a park, rail and subway... The budget runs into eye-watering sums of money.

Glancing through the list of shareholders I see, as expected, Richard Haswell 51%, Alexander Thornton, 25%, Jaye Thornton, 10%, followed by a long list of minor shareholders whose names I do not recognise but believe to be perhaps engineers, designers or architects working for share rather than fee. I notice that Francis has 1%. Coming to the end of the list, I sit bolt upright.

Elizabeth Kimberley 2%

*****

I didn't say before, Elizabeth, but nice bed. Good choice," says my Master approvingly, as he pushes me down over the foot of the mattress, bending me forward, face down, arms outstretched. He shackles me with the handcuffs to the bedposts, then pushes my feet apart with his. Another pair of cuffs snaps around my left ankle, and then my right, spreading my legs further.

The bed is of wrought iron, metal bars at foot and head, handily available as anchors for ropes, scarves or chains. I chose it carefully for my apartment, for its beauty, and for utility in the games my Master and I enjoy.

He reaches around and below me, working away at the laces of my bodice, gradually teasing the garment apart, allowing my breasts to hang free, enfolded in the curtain of my long red hair. Pinching gently at a nipple, he rolls it between finger and thumb and I wince, but at the same time, a thrill skitters through me, connecting with my pussy, nerves jumping at both ends. Flushing, I gnaw my lip.

"Nice and gently tonight, I think, Elizabeth. You took enough punishment last time."

I have to agree. Exhilarating as it was at the time, I still have the red marks of the riding crop decorating my rear end. My Master traces their outline with his fingers, then trails down and in, caressing my folds, already moist with anticipation.

He strokes my thighs, outside, then working in, making me squirm with pleasure. He makes no attempt to prevent my movement, but since I am spreadeagled anyway, it makes little difference.

My colour is rising with arousal, face and pussy blushing, belly and breasts flushing red, glistening.

"You look beautiful, Elizabeth. Ripe and ready for me." My Master, kneeling, kisses me, barely touching me, on the pussy. His tongue passes over me, so lightly, almost not there. The effect is electrifying. "And you taste wonderful too."

His fingers skim over and past my clit, making me stretch and arch for more, but his hands and mouth have moved on.

Strong hands massage my shoulders, my back, and down past my waist, curving over the length of my spine, the dimples in the small of my back. Hands linger over the line of waist into hip, stomach to thighs. Fingers wind through my red curls, briefly gliding over my erect clit, then onward.

A single finger slips between my pussy lips, gliding like silk through and away.

Everything is transient. I *ache* for a prolonged caress; for my Master to work me, to fuck me. Instead, artist that he is, he paints a portrait of growing arousal over my whole body. Every touch is fleeting; barely there before it is instantly gone.

"Please, Master..."

"Not yet."

"*Please...*"

"No." And his exquisite foreplay continues.

His warm breath playing over my pussy leaves me straining to move closer to him, to draw him into me. I want him to taste me, to drink from me, to raise me to climax.

Instead, his teasing of my every nerve-ending continues. He strokes the back of my knees, the tender skin inside my arms and my thighs. Leaning over me, he nibbles gently at my ears and neck. Hands stroke the curve of my pendulous breasts, supporting their heaviness in cupped palms. Fingers tease at my nipples, now crinkling hard, tinted rose against my pale skin. As he leans over me, I can feel his erection through his jeans, pressed against my back and I long to have him inside me, filling me...

"Master, please. I need to cum."

"No."

"Please, Master. Please."

A finger slips into my pussy, and I clamp convulsively around it, only to find it withdrawn. Then two fingers enter, my pussy throbbing reflexively around them. Again, they are withdrawn. A hand slides below me, and between, teasing at my clit, and I gasp and buck.

"You *do* need to cum, don't you?"

Oh God...

"Master, please..."

There is a moment's pause and looking backwards through my curtain of hair, I see him shucking off his jeans, peeling off his shirt, shaft erect against his flat abdomen.

He is so beautiful. Lean, yet broad-shouldered, biceps strap-like under his skin, and a fine line of dark hair tracing down from his belly to his groin. His deep blue eyes are intense with passion and lust.

Standing behind and over me, a hand either side of my hips, he positions himself between my manacled ankles, testing me.

The tip of his erection kisses against my dripping pussy, pressing so lightly, making my inner muscles jump and spasm against him, then slowly he sheathes himself, gently, so gently, inside me. Not thrusting, not moving, simply inside me, filling me. Full length he enters, his balls resting against my lips. I hear him draw breath as he fights for his own control.

Aroused through I am, my pussy swollen, dripping and hot, still he stretches me as he enters.

I groan and shiver, thinking that now he will pump me, but he does not. I want him to fuck me, hard. I want him to fuck my brains out. Instead, his arms curve around to embrace me, one hand opening my pussy lips from the front, the other taking my clit between thumb and finger.

"Watch," he says and from my face-down position, I watch as, with the smallest of movements, he manipulates my bud, sliding back the hood to release the sensitive heart.

I see his fingers, wet and slippery with my pussy juices, work at me. The movements are so small, but they are electrifying. Sweet fire radiates from my clit, waves of unbearable pleasure rippling through me.

Still, he does not thrust. Instead, he revolves his hips, grinding against me, pressing against my G-spot, back and forth, knowing exactly where I can best feel him inside me.

Unable to remain still, I heave and strain and writhe, but am pinned by wrists, ankles, and now also speared on my Master's cock.

Whilst not thrusting, he can surely feel my convulsions as he flicks and rolls and slides my clit with his fingers. As my body struggles against this exquisite pleasure-torture, he leans his weight against me, restraining me further, pressing into my liquid inner, pinning my movements.

Panting for breath, my pulse pounding, "Are you going to cum for me now, Elizabeth?" he whispers.

"Yes, Master".

Abso-fuckin-lutely Master.

My words emerge broken, piece by piece as my orgasm arises gradually, blooming outwards from my heated core. Pulsating pleasure ripples through my belly and my Master presses hard with one flat hand, my belly muscles against his penis, still hard inside me.

As I moan, my spasms seem to trigger his as, his face next to mine, he gasps and trembles. Now he pumps, thrusting two, three, four times, before driving against my inner walls, spurting into me.

His hand still pressing flat against my stomach, his spasms and my own, ripple through our enmeshed bodies, our groans and cries mingling in combined release, my juices and his flowing freely down my thighs.

For a few seconds, he collapses onto me, his face resting next to mine, and I am taking his full body weight, my wrists and ankles straining against their restraints. Then he remembers himself and, kissing me on the cheek, lifts away from me.

"Thank you, Elizabeth."

"Thank you, Master."

*****

Later, showered, clean and comfortable, we lie together on my bed, drinking wine, discussing everything and nothing in the candlelight.

"Master, there's something I think I need to tell you about."

Cocking an eyebrow at me, "Oh? What?".

"You know Mack Kane?"

"What about him? He lost his job when you spotted that he'd been defrauding the company."

"Yes, but... I've seen him a few times since then. I think he's following me."

My Master looks appalled. "What! When was this?"

"Usually when I'm coming home from the office. I keep seeing him and I wonder if he's trying to find out where I live now. The first time I thought it was just a coincidence, but it's kept happening. I think I've managed to lose him in the crowds each time but..."

He holds up a warding hand. "Say no more, Elizabeth. I'll get right onto it. I think a prohibition order is needed. I have friends within the police. We'll get it fast-tracked for you."

"Thank you, Master."

"I'm sorry, Elizabeth. You don't deserve this."

"It's alright, Master. It's not your fault. I didn't want to bother you with it but..."

He jabs a finger at me. "This is the kind of thing you *do* bother me with. If anything else happens, you tell me right away. I mean that. You call me *immediately*. You have my mobile number, and I'll tell Francis to make sure that if you call the office, it comes straight through to me if you say it's important."

"Alright. I'll do that."

He stretches and yawns. "I'm sorry, Elizabeth, but I have to go. I have a lot on tomorrow and the following day, so it could be the end of the week before I see you again. But don't worry about things. I'll contact the police tomorrow morning. And you keep in touch if you need to. I wouldn't forgive myself if anything were to happen to you. Alright?"

I nod. "That's fine, Master."

"Good night, Elizabeth." He kisses me, softly, on the lips, his hand caressing my hair.

Quickly dressing, he leaves, clicking the door closed behind him. I start making myself ready for sleep; a cup of tea, a book, soft music, when I see my Master's briefcase on the couch.

Buzzing down to the concierge, "Sorry, Miss Kimberley. He's already left the building. About five minutes ago."

Undecided, I hover...

Should I call him at this late hour? He said he's busy tomorrow, so he probably needs the case.

I *could* message Ross, the driver, to call by and pick it up first thing in the morning...

Yes, that's the right thing to do.

I am just tapping out a text when the door buzzes.

Ah!

He's realized that he left it behind and has returned to collect it.

"Coming..." I shout and go to the door to unlock it.

As the lock snaps up, the door crashes open in my face and a man bursts in. Stepping backwards, Mack Kane slams me against the wall, his hands around my throat.

The Story Continues in 'The Master's Heart'

Part Eight
The Master's Heart

...The door bursts open and Mack Kane slams me against the wall and down, his hands around my throat.

I have no time to be frightened, only to react. He is not a large man, but he is still stronger and more powerful than I am. Gasping and choking, I cannot fight him off. I am trying, with both hands, to break his grip on my neck, but the momentum of his charge through the door has pushed me to the floor, and he has the advantage now of height; his weight bearing down on me.

"You little bitch!" he yells. "You think you could do that and get away with it? You think you're so fucking *clever...*"

I cannot break loose. He is strangling me, and my vision is beginning to blur. I cannot breathe. The hot blackness of unconsciousness circles in on me.

"Bitch!" he screams. "*Bitch!* I'll teach you!"

My knees start to collapse under me. I have no air, and the darkness is taking me...

"What the *Hell* do you think you're doing?"

Abruptly, my attacker is pulled loose from me, his hands releasing their hold on my throat, and I collapse to the floor, gagging for breath... Crying... Sobbing...

I think I'm going to be sick...

It is my Master. He has returned, and not a moment too soon. As I gasp on the floor, chest heaving, the two men struggle by the doorway. Suddenly Mack breaks free and dashes out of the door. Through blurry vision I see my Master hesitate, clearly wanting to follow, but not wanting to leave me. He drops to the floor beside me.

I'm still on hands and knees, coughing and crying, tears streaming down my face. Now the adrenaline has had time to kick in, and I am shaking, trembling, sucking in huge lungs-full of air, sobs racking my frame. My Master, cradles me in his arms, rocking me.

"Elizabeth. Oh God, Elizabeth. I'm so sorry. I shouldn't have left you. Oh, God. I could have lost you. I could have lost you."

Choking out some words through my tears and shaking. "I'm alright, really, Master. I'm alright."

"No, you're *not.* How *can* you be alright? You were attacked. He was trying to kill you." He sits me on the floor, my back against the wall, one hand flat on my chest, the other caressing my face.

"I'll only be a moment. Don't move." Striding to the intercom, he dials the contact for the concierge. "Yes, an ambulance. And the police. Right now. And close up the building. Seal all the doors. Don't let him get out. Don't argue! *NOW!*"

He yells the final words, before stabbing the connection closed.

I have to pull myself together. My Master is normally so self-controlled, so magnificent. To see him like this is upsetting beyond words. I must calm myself, and so calm him. I have not been seriously hurt, only shaken, and Mack will soon be arrested and locked up. My Master knows people and Mack will not get away with this. I did nothing to him except, accidentally, expose his fraud.

"Master, please, calm down. I'm alright. Truly, he hasn't hurt me. It was mainly the shock."

I draw in deep breaths, forcing myself to relax, willing my hammering heartbeat to slow down, and hoping that my aching throat is not the sign of anything more serious than bruises.

As my breathing eases, my Master visibly relaxes. But almost engulfing me in his embrace, he kisses my forehead, rocking me in a kind of circular motion that suggests he is comforting himself as much as me.

Sirens wail and blue light flashes up through the windows, into the room. It's weird, unearthly, and I feel sort of disconnected, spaced out...

... and...

*****

... I wake in bed, disoriented, staring up at a ceiling.

This is not my bedroom.

Where am I?

After a moment's hesitation, I sit up.

Ah, this is my Master's bedroom, and he sits close by in a large armchair, writing notes. As I stir, he looks up, smiling. "Ah, Elizabeth. You're awake. How do you feel?"

How do I feel?

A bit fuzzy still.

"I'm alright. I think. Have I been asleep long?"

"For a while. Don't worry about it. Coffee perhaps? Something to eat?"

"Mmmm, yes. That would be lovely."

"I'll make the coffee and ring down for some food. What would you like?"

"Oh, just something light. Soup perhaps."

"Coming up."

Five minutes later he returns bearing a tray with coffee pot. "I've ordered you some soup. There are a couple of people out there who need to see you."

"Oh?"

"There's a doctor here. He examined you while you slept, and thinks you are basically unharmed, but he wants to check you over now while he can talk to you. Also, do you feel up to giving a statement to the police?"

"Yes, I think so."

The doctor comes in and asks me a lot of questions. Does it hurt when I move my neck? Do I have any tingling in my fingers? Does my breathing feel normal? He concludes that I am as well as can be expected and was mainly suffering from shock.

The police officer who questions me is a woman. She is mostly interested in the details of the attack itself, such as they are, and says that there will be other officers later to inquire as to the details of Mack Kane's fraud.

There is, of course, very little I can tell her. The whole thing happened so quickly. But I do tell her about Mack having followed me for some days prior to the event. The whole thing makes me shudder, and I don't want to think about it anymore. I am glad when she goes.

My Master shows her out and then sits beside me again. "I've sent Ross over with Francis to collect some of your things. I want you to stay here for at least the next few days until Mack is tracked down. That way I can keep an eye on you. Is that okay with you?"

The chance to *stay* with him for several days? "Of course it is, Master. But I thought you had a lot of work on?"

"Fuck the work. This is more important. And I can do a lot of it from here anyway."

Then the penny drops as to what my Master just said. "Tracked down? They didn't catch him?"

He hesitates. "No, I'm sorry, Elizabeth. He escaped the building before they were able to lock it down. But don't worry. He'll be found."

I ponder this, gulping at the implications of Mack Kane loose in the city. But does my Master really want me to stay with him? He's never wanted me to stay for long before.

"I'll be fine in a couple of days, Master. It won't have to be for long."

He raises a quizzical eyebrow at me. "Don't you want to stay here? Don't you like the idea of living with me?"

"Of course I do. But I didn't think that..."

He takes my hand, holding it between his. "This has made me realise Elizabeth how close we have become, you and I. When I came in, and I saw Mack with his hands around your throat, you on the floor, I thought my heart would stop. And I only returned by chance, because I'd forgotten my briefcase. If I hadn't..." His voice chokes and he looks away.

"But you *did* come back. And I'm fine. Please, Master, don't get upset." I bend to kiss the hands encasing mine, and his eyes sweep up to meet me, depthless with emotion. Rising from his chair, he moves to sit on the bed beside me, holding my face in his hands as he kisses me.

My breath comes in a rush, the kiss sending a tremble through me. His face is rough. He has not shaved, and the stubble rubs against my skin. It does not matter. This is my Master and I want him. As my heat rises, there is a familiar moistening between my legs and I wrap my arms around his shoulders, pulling him closer.

He resists, looking at me a little startled. "Are you sure that you're ready for this, Elizabeth?"

I am always ready for him. "Yes, Master. I am. Please, I want you close to me."

A slow smile curves his lips, his eyes crinkling at the edges, and he shakes his head, chuckling. "She's just been near strangled, and *still* she's horny."

Then his hands sweep down to tug at my nightgown. "Well, as my Lady wishes. I think *this* is surplus to need." He tugs upwards, lifting the garment over my head, leaving me naked in the bed. "Lie back, Elizabeth. You're not going to be doing anything strenuous today."

I obey, arranging myself enticingly on the sheets. My Master strips off in an almost business-like fashion, holding my gaze as he does so, then lies beside me.

He is tender, warm, his eyes soft as he kisses me. Stroking the side of my face and my hair, he winds his fingers through my copper tresses, then leans over me to nuzzle a breast, gently sucking at a nipple.

His touch is, as ever, magical. Sighing, I stroke his hair as he suckles me. The scent of him close to me, skin on skin, is musky, heady, and I inhale deeply, breathing him in.

Slowly he slips down my body, kissing the soft skin of my stomach, exploring my thighs with his fingertips before working through my curls, and within.

His touch on my bud is so light, so delicate, and yet it ignites me. Sighing, I arch my back, spreading my legs for him, giving him what is his. He explores my warm, damp folds, my breathing becoming rapid and uneven, my hips beginning to judder and twitch.

"Oh, Master..." I almost breathe the words.

"Yes?"

"It's wonderful."

"Lie back, Elizabeth. Relax."

Easing himself between my legs, he kisses and licks the soft skin of my thighs, working upwards and in, leaving me brimming with a tingling anticipation. Kissing my warm folds, he nestles into my sex, lapping at me, his tongue circling and probing inwards whilst one finger continues its work on my clit.

I am warming from within, liquefying for him. Everything I have is for my Master, and I *want* him.

Tenderly, he slips back the hood of my clit, flicking with the tip of his tongue at the hardening tip within, making me gasp. My hips quiver as he parts my swelling lips, tasting me. My pussy runs hot and liquid, and as he laps at me, long slow strokes up and through and over my clit, I moan and curve up to meet him.

His fingers slide inside my slick entrance, penetrating only slowly and I whimper, desperate for more, but desperate for this to last. The fingers venture inside me again, harder this time, and my inner muscles shiver and clench. Pushing in deeply, he rubs up against my G-spot, and now I wail my arousal; a noise from deep within me as I quake and tremble. Desire pulses through me, and I want to be filled.

"Master, please, I want you inside me."

"Not yet."

"Please."

"No. Not yet. I am still the Master here, and I say, not *yet.*"

The fingers withdraw, slipping up to my clit. His mouth clamps around me, tongue pushing into my brimming sex, circling inside, licking me out, and I howl.

My hips bucking, the tongue in my cunt sends pulsating pleasure rippling over my belly and thighs. My clit is almost electrically alive, sending sparks of irresistible arousal throbbing through me.

My climax is rising, welling up from within. Arching up my pelvis on quivering legs, I tremble and shake as, irresistibly, the rush takes me. As I scream ecstatically, my Master holds me at the hips, still working me as waves of pulsating orgasm radiate out from my core.

My climax subsides, but as I relax, my Master pulls free of me, pressing me down to the sheets with a hand flat on my belly.

As he kneels up for a moment, I see his throbbing erection, taut and hard against his flat stomach, twitching to a pulse-beat. Lowering himself down over me, he nudges at my entrance with his shaft before easing slowly in.

He tests me a few times, in and out, gradually opening my already engorged and wet entrance, stretching me wide to accommodate him. As he does so, he holds my eyes for a moment, then kisses me on the lips, soft flesh on flesh, tongue-tip tasting at me. He tastes sweet, clean. Closing my eyes, I run my fingers through his hair, scenting him, reveling in his lovemaking, and the afterglow of my orgasm.

He loves me.

I see it in his face as he looks at me, but he won't say the words.

Why not?

He slides in and out, my cunt involuntarily constricting around him, holding him tight as he fucks me. Slowly he moves, working me, and I see in his grimace that he is fighting for control, his own climax hovering. Biting his lower lip, with the slowest of movements, he sheathes himself, over and again, in my molten core.

Unbidden, I feel it rising again. My Master's cock deep inside me, my inner muscles judder and pulsate as, once more, orgasm laps at my shores and then, in cascading waves, rushes through me. I cry out, reaching up to hold my Master, my nails biting into his back, and through a haze of erotic pleasure, I feel and hear his own control fail, and he Comes. Pressing hard against my walls, he bucks as he spurts into me, my climax and his, uniting us in the shared moment.

He drops onto me with a gasp. I lie, utterly passive; completely spent by my double orgasm.

For a long minute, we lie together in silence, he still deep inside me.

Finally, he speaks. "That was amazing." Taking a deep breath, he withdraws and pulls himself up, kneeling between my sprawled thighs. His still twitching cock beats a merry heartbeat, and there is joy in his eyes. "We've really got something haven't we, Elizabeth?"

"Yes, Master. I think we have... Master?"

"Hmmm?"

"I'm hungry."

He bursts out laughing. "I'm not surprised. Shall I order something? I think you should stay in bed still."

"Yes, Master, that's fine."

"Good." He gets up and puts on a bathrobe. "I'm going for a shower. Oh..." He pulls something from the pocket of the robe. "You'd better have this too." He tosses it to me and reflexively, I catch it. A key. I look at it in puzzlement, then to my Master.

"It's a key to this apartment," he explains. "If you're going to be living here, you'd better be able to get in."

*****

I spend the rest of the week in a dreamy haze. After a couple of days in bed, I feel fine and am bored rigid. Against my Master's protests, I return to work.

But I am thinking hard.

I know my Master loves me. I see it in his face, and he shows it by his actions if not his words.

I continue my work with the Thornton deal, familiarizing myself with as much of it as I can. Jaye and Alex Thornton both seem to like me, and my Master, 'Richard' at these meetings, always brings me along, saying that my presence makes the negotiations go more smoothly.

My sun is shining, and my skies are blue.

Turning the key in the lock, I click open the door to my Master's apartment and walk in, calling as I enter. "Hi, it's only me..." Then I freeze at the tableau I see before me.

My Master is there, in the lounge and Adele, his 'ex', is with him. She is wearing a very short scarlet dress with deeply plunging neckline. Her long dark hair is swinging loosely around her, and she is pressed up close to my Master, arms around his neck, kissing him.

As I stand there, gaping, she turns her face to me, almost sneering, a sneer that turns to triumph as she sees me.

My Master calls out. "Elizabeth..." But I turn and run, sick to the pit of my stomach, trying to keep back the tears until I can cry in private. Taking the lift down to the lobby, I keep my face down as I make for the door. The phone rings in my pocket, but I ignore it.

A minute later there is the *Bing* of a text arriving. Then another. I ignore both, instead hailing a taxi to take me to my own apartment.

Slamming the door closed behind me, I finally allow myself to collapse into tears, letting the sobs rack me as I grieve. How could he have done that to me? I trusted him. He even encouraged me to live with him. And then to have *her* there...

My phone rings again. Checking the screen, it is Richard calling me, and this time I decide to answer.

"Elizabeth. We have to talk. That wasn't what..."

I don't want to hear it.

I hang up.

Miserably, I wonder what to do with myself and settle for pouring myself a drink, a large drink. It will make me tipsy, but that's probably not a bad idea right now. Gulping it down, I pour myself another and then, cradling the glass, I stand by the window, staring out over the cityscape far below, feeling wretched. The tears have stopped flowing and for some time I stand there; just stand.

The intercom buzzes. "Elizabeth. It's Richard. Let me in."

I do not answer. I don't want to talk to him.

"Elizabeth. Open this door. We need to talk."

I don't reply.

"Elizabeth. I know you're in there. The concierge told me you're here. Now let me in."

Still, I say nothing.

For a moment there is silence and then, with a crash, the door bursts open as my Master kicks it in.

Startled, I jump backwards, pressing myself against the wall. He strides into the room, looking volcanically angry.

I wave a finger at the door, lock broken, wood splintered. "The door..."

"I *own* this building. It's *my* fucking door. I'll replace it." he snarls. Striding over, he jabs a finger towards me. "I know you're upset, Elizabeth, but there are some things you *don't* do, and one of them is to hang up on me."

He snatches the glass from my hand and puts it on the coffee table. Seizing me by the shoulders, he pushes me against the wall. Never have I seen him like this before. This is a side of my Master I did not even suspect existed. Still holding me by the shoulders, he shakes me.

"Don't you *ever* do that again! If you have something to say, then *say* it. But don't *ever* put the phone down on me. Do we understand each other?"

He continues. "I'm sorry you saw what you did, but I told you weeks ago that Adele is out of my life..."

"You were kissing her..."

"No. *She* was kissing *me*. There's a difference. And if you had stayed another ten seconds, you would have seen me push her off, and order her out of my apartment."

Dumbly, I nod. And bizarrely, I realise that, apart from owing an apology to my Master for my bad manners, I am not frightened of him, even in this mood. Although my breathing is rapid, it is not from fear. As he pushes me against the wall, my panties are getting wet.

"Do you have anything more that you would like to ask?" he says. "Or can I take it that you're going to behave like a normal human being now?" Then he pauses, looks at me closely, tilting his head, and chuckles. "I don't believe it! You're getting off on this, aren't you?"

I nod, looking down, embarrassed, but he lifts up my chin with a finger. "I thought I'd scared you for a minute there, but you're panting, and you've got eyes like saucers. Well, you don't get away with it that easily, Madam."

He releases my shoulders but instead curls the fingers of both hands into the buttons of my blouse and tugs it open. Buttons pop in all directions and fabric rips as he pulls the remains of the garment off me.

I start to protest. "My clothes..."

He interrupts. "Fuck the clothes. It's one of the perks of being rich, Elizabeth. I can easily pay for more." And with that he unzips my skirt, ripping it open the rest of the way, dropping what's left to the floor to join the shredded remains of my blouse, leaving me only in black lace bra and panties.

I gasp, my pussy flooding.

With one hand he yanks at the front of my bra, and the fastenings simply pop open under this mistreatment. My breasts swing free as he rips it from me, and his free hand grabs a nipple, pinching hard. I yelp, but he continues, looking me in the eye. "Girls with bad manners get punished for it. Now..."

He pauses reflectively, looking down at my panties and hooking them around the top with a finger. "Do we think these are needed now?" He slips a finger into my crotch, feeling at the fabric. "Nope. Useless. As I suspected. Sopping wet. So, they can go." And he tears the fragile fabric, ripping the panties off me.

"Now, Madam. Down you go. No, not onto your knees. I want your butt up where I can get at it."

He pushes me down, bending me over double, hands on the floor to support myself, almost touching my toes. "You can spread those too." He pushes my ankles apart with his feet.

"Now..." He slaps a butt-cheek hard with one hand. "Repeat after me. 'I will not be rude to my Master.'"

I giggle. "I will not be rude to my Master."

He slaps again, the other cheek. It stings and I yelp.

He continues. "My Master does not lie to me."

I sober up at this, at what he is telling me. "My Master does not lie to me."

Slap. My pussy is streaming, and hot liquid runs down inside my thighs.

"My Master will punish me if I am rude to him." *Slap!*

"My Master will punish me if I am rude to him."

Slap! This time, the stroke is not on the cheeks of my butt, but on my engorging pussy and I squeal. My Master takes no notice. "My Master is going to fuck my brains out as a punishment."

I start to wriggle, trying both escape from and embrace the sting of my butt cheeks and the hot glow in my pussy. "My Master is going to fuck my brains out as a punishment."

Slap! "I'm still being bad by being so wet, that my Master's cock is going to float inside me..."

I try to repeat but a fit of giggles takes over, and my arms give way at the elbow.

Slap! "Did I say you could move?"

"I'm sorry, Master. I can't keep my balance."

Slap! "You may support yourself on the coffee table."

Obediently I move to place my hands on the coffee table, supporting myself more firmly as my Master seizes me by the hips, and arranges my ass and my dripping cunt to his satisfaction.

Slap!

It really smarts now. The strikes are hard, and getting harder, but my pussy lips are hot and engorged, juices dripping freely.

Abruptly, he reaches around in front of me, pinching my clit between two fingers. It is too much, and I yell out...

Bbbzzzz....

The intercom. "Hey, Beth. You okay up there? A neighbor said there was some noise."

My Master falls still and silent.

The heat in my cunt blooming outward, my clit incandescent with pain-pleasure, I struggle to get the words out, shouting across to the intercom. "Er, yes, fine. Don't worry. I... Er... I just dropped something."

"Okay. So long as you're alright."

"Yeah, thanks."

"Don't move. I've not finished with you." His words are stern, but my Master's voice is brimming with laughter as he steps over to the intercom and clicks it off. Sliding over a chair, he jams the smashed door closed, pushing the chair-back under what is left of the handle. Then he vanishes into my bedroom, returning a minute later with a handful of my stockings.

Coming back to me, he grabs a handful of my hair and hauls me upright. "You. Dining table. Bend over and spread 'em." He marches me over to the table, pushes me face down and stretches my arms out, tying each wrist to a table leg with a stocking. Then he does the same with my ankles. Halfway through, he pauses to grab a cushion, shoving it under my hips, arching my back and raising my butt. The ankle ties he stretches tight, spreading me wide, and displaying my swollen and sopping slit.

Face pressed to the tabletop, I cannot move and, hair draped over my face, I cannot see.

I hear movement, rustling...

My Master getting undressed and...

Something else - he is moving around the apartment...

Looking for something?

The bang of cupboard doors and drawers opening and shutting...

The click of my bedroom door...

Then my office door...

His footsteps come close. His hand sweeps the hair from my face.

"I thought you should see what was coming," he says, dangling something in front of me. "We never got around to trying this one out, did we?"

From my awkward angle, I make out the shape of the riding crop I bought him for his Birthday.

A *frisson* runs through me, and my slit pumps out hot fluid.

"And these are for some other parts of you." He shows me a handful of bulldog clips. "Let's see how far we can go before that wet cunt of yours has had enough."

His footsteps are behind me now. Something brushes against me from behind. The tip of the riding crop? It probes my lips, pushing first to one side, then the other, inserting itself as it goes. It pushes inside, not deeply, but enough that, in my highly sensitized state, I screech in response. It withdraws instantly.

"None of that," comes my Master's voice. "We don't want any more interruptions."

Footsteps again. He crosses the room, returning with something. The *something* dangles by my face again... My panties?

Or what's left of them.

"Open wide."

I obey, and the panties, tasting of my own juices, are shoved in my mouth.

"Now," continues my Master. "You can't speak, and you can't yell. And I'm going to give it to you hard this time. Much as I love you, you really pissed me off earlier. I know you didn't like what you saw, but you gave me no chance to speak. And *that's* not fair. So, this time, *I'm* not going to be fair. You have no safe word, and *I'm* going to decide when you've had enough. Do you understand?"

My heart pounds. Through the muffle of the gagging panties, I *Mmmmph* an acknowledgement.

But my head is spinning...

My Master said that he loves me.

But... He going to punish me. *Really* punish me.

For the first time since I have known him, I am scared. Exhilarated and nervous. Joyous and frightened.

I *know* he will do me no real harm. But I also understand, very clearly, that he is going to take me to my limits.

Something clamps onto one of my pussy lips, stretching it open to one side, and through the panties, I yell. One mercy; gagged as I am, I can scream as loud as I like.

With a snap, the other engorged lip is clipped into place.

"Mmmm. Should I do the third clip as well, I wonder?" His tongue runs up the length of me, over my aching clit and through, into my wide-stretched cunt. "Delicious!" Then the third clip snaps over my clit. It is excruciating, and I scream through the gag.

"Enjoying that?" My Master's hand reaches under the left-hand side of my chest, pressing for a minute. "And your heart rate is about one-fifty beats a minute I'd say. I think we can ramp it up further."

There is a pause and more sound of movement. "Now then, Elizabeth. You do have one choice. I can either warn you when it's coming, or it can be a surprise. Which is it to be? Flap your left hand for a warning, or your right hand for a surprise."

I hesitate, then flap my left hand.

"Alright. Here it comes. Three, two, one."

Thwack!

The crop comes down on my left buttock. I try to shriek through the gag, jerk and struggle against the white-hot pain, and then,

"Three, two, one."

Thwack!

I need to scream. I need to breathe. But the gag stops me doing either. The pain on my clipped pussy lips and clit is agonising, but nonetheless, waves of arousal are pulsating through my cunt.

"Three, two, one..."

I tense, trying to deny what is coming, but at the same time, wanting more, somehow disconnected from reality.

Thwack!

Tears run down my face. I feel spaced out, but fantastic. The contradiction of the pain of my body, and the pleasure within leaves me dreamy, lost.

My Master's face swings into my field of vision, and he gazes levelly at me for a moment, then disappears from view once more.

"Three, two, one."

Thwack!

I can take no more. Limply, I lie on the table, twitching with pain and arousal. Magically, there's no more until, with a snap, the clips are pulled off and agony ripples through me, followed closely by the hot breath of my Master close to me before he clamps his mouth over my pussy and licks me out.

I have no warning. No build-up. I simply orgasm.

My jerking, twitching body flops on the table in its restraints. My cunt spasms and pulses, and my Master does not stop. Mercilessly, he probes, and slurps and sucks, drinking my gushing juices as I cum into his mouth. He continues on and on, mouthing my lips, chewing my folds. The orgasm lasts and stretches, and I squeal like a madwoman, struggling pointlessly against my gag and bindings.

Finally, he pulls away from me, only to plunge in deep with his cock, spearing me hard, banging against me inside, his balls swinging against my sore clit. He pumps and pounds inside me; clasping my hips as he fucks me. Through the connection to his hands, I feel his own on-coming release; the build to the rush.

The grasp of his hands becomes painful, and his orgasm, when it comes, is violent, savage. His cries and groans are loud as with a spurt of heat I feel inside myself, he shoots into me, bending forward over my back as he does so, seizing my hard nipples and squeezing hard as his hips grind against me.

With a yell, he pulls out of me, slapping a buttock as he does so. Our mixed juices trickle down inside my legs, as he walks around and pulls the panties out of my mouth. Stooping, he looks me in the eyes, "Was *that* enough of a ride for you, Madam?"

My tongue and mouth are dry, fluffy and it takes me a moment to assemble enough saliva to speak. My face still pressed against the tabletop. "That's a *Hell* of a way to decide to tell me that you love me."

He gawps at me then, his eyes softening, he runs one hand through my hair, and with the other, tugs the knots free from my wrists. Kneeling down, he releases my ankles, but as I try to stand, my knees give.

Catching me on the way down, he scoops me up and, carrying me through to the bedroom, lays me on the bed. I yelp as the weals on my butt make contact with the covers. Rolling onto my side and looking back into the mirror, I can see red stripes over my otherwise creamy skin.

My Master, still naked, sits beside me on the bed, resting his head on his chin. Looking slantways at me, he says "But you know that I love you? Surely?"

"But you wouldn't say so, Master."

He is silent, reflective, then, taking my hand, he kisses the fingers. "Elizabeth, for the avoidance of doubt, I love you. I want you to be with me. I want you to be part of my life."

A warm glow suffuses through me.

"I love you too, Master."

The Story Continues in 'The Master's Rage.'

Part Nine
The Master's Rage

I'm tired of studying. Although I have exams next week and need to revise, my brain and eyes are tired. I can feel myself growing stale almost by the minute.

My Master sits opposite me, working, legs crossed at the ankle, examining papers and accounts, making occasional notes in the margin. Bored with reading about economics, budgets, surplus and deficits, financial accounting versus cost accounting, and...

Time for a change of tone...

Plucking a grape from the bunch on the table next to me, I toss it at my Master. It bounces off his file, and down onto the settee beside him.

Over his glasses, he gazes expressionlessly at me for a moment, picks up the grape, pops it in his mouth, and returns to his note making.

Piqued at such a non-response, I pluck and toss another grape. This time it lands on his lap. Once again, he levels a look at me and pops it in his mouth. "I thought you were supposed to be working?" he says. "Studying hard for your exams?"

"Well, yes, but I'm tired. I need a break."

"*You* need a break, so I have to be disturbed while I am trying to work?"

"You've been at it for hours too. Don't you want a rest as well?"

"I need to get this done for the meeting with the Thorntons tomorrow."

"You'll perform better at the meeting if you're rested."

"Later, Elizabeth. Right now, I must finish this." And he returns to his reading.

I wait for a minute, then toss a third grape at him. This time he, somehow, catches it one-handedly in mid-air, apparently without even looking at it.

As he puts it in his mouth he says, "If you keep this up, I'll put you over my knee and spank your ass red."

At his words, my panties suddenly become moist with heat. With a take a sharp intake of breath, I now know what *kind* of break I'm looking for.

Deciding that grapes as a tactic are passé, I wheel out the big guns.

Silently, stretching back in my chair like a cat, I start to trace the outline of my breasts, trailing fingers over my contours, waiting for my Master to notice. Irritatingly, he appears to be unaware of what I am doing.

Vexed, I hitch up my skirt a little and part my knees, displaying rather more thigh, and revealing a slight view of my panties. This time, my Master notices the movements and glances up briefly, before, doing a double take, he looks up properly, staring, as I return to playing with my breasts.

Cupping myself through my blouse, I have my Master's attention. No longer looking at his files, his eyes instead follow my fingers as they draw circles around the outline of my nipples whereas they harden, they begin to display through the fabric. My nipples, responding, pucker up under the attention they are receiving, displaying hard little nubs through the silky material.

My questing fingers trail down between breasts, stomach and thighs, ever lower towards the hem of my skirt. Slipping under and in, they trace a line along the inside of my thighs to the green silk of my panties.

My Master watches transfixed, his work abandoned beside him. Sitting with arms folded, legs outstretched, he watches my performance, his black jeans beginning to bulge noticeably, and my own underwear becoming ever damper.

Enjoying this feeling of erotic power over my Master, I continue, running fingers over and around my sex and clit, massaging myself through the sheer fabric, all the while, watching his reactions. His eyes are level, pupils wide and dark. For a moment, they meet mine, before eye-pointing downwards, indicating that I should continue.

Sliding inside the panties, I play with my clit, gently tormenting my warming bud, allowing the contour of my moving fingers to be outlined through the silk, as a dark wet stain spreads across the fabric. His head tilts a little as he watches this, before saying "Get rid of them."

"Master?"

"Your panties. Get rid of them."

Obediently, I rise, slide out of the garment and start to sit again."

"No, not there." My Master points to the other end of the settee on which he is sitting. "*There,* Madam, if you would. If you insist on flaunting yourself, I'll have a good view, thank you."

Arranging myself on the end of the couch, I raise a leg, allowing my Master to see everything that is his. It is not entirely coincidental, that now I am in this position, it will be very easy for my Master to lean forward to reach me. Perhaps it will be with his tongue.

However, he shows no sign of doing this yet. Instead, he has swung around, watching me in silence. Adjusting my position to ensure that he has the best possible view, I face him, thighs akimbo, fully displayed.

My blouse seems also surplus to need, so slowly, I undo each button, letting the garment fall open, before sliding it from my shoulders and letting it fall away. My green lacy bra goes the same way. Unclipping it, I allow my large, pendulous breasts to swing free, nipples now hard, rosy and crinkled with arousal.

Cupping a breast, and licking my fingers, I tease at the nipple, hardening it further. Plucking and rolling, I ensure that my Master can see what I am doing at all times, his view uninterrupted. His eyes indicate I should give the other side similar attention, so changing around, I lift and caress the other breast, again tormenting the nipple into taut attention.

Now, naked except for my skirt, I want to draw my Master into some action.

I want to be *fucked.*

Running fingers over my thighs, stroking inwards, slipping through red curls to neatly trimmed pussy lips, I open myself up, parting moist and swelling folds to reveal my dripping core.

The bulge in my Master's jeans is unmistakable now. As I dip fingers into my wet pussy, slipping them rhythmically in and out, a sheen of sweat develops on his forehead.

I am also perspiring heavily, droplets hovering between my breasts, as my heart begins to race. Finger fucking myself, I keep my thumb pressed against my pulsing clit.

Oh, God, Master. Please...

*I want **you** to do this.*

His self-control fails and he almost launches himself towards me, ready to bury his face in my sex, when...

Bbbbbbzzzzzzz...

The door intercom...

My Master and I speak simultaneously. "Fuck!"

"Oh, fuck!"

A voice comes over the tannoy. "Richard? It's Francis. I have those figures you requested, and a file from Jaye Thornton with the marketing projections."

My Master's eyes roll heavenwards, then fasten on mine in apology. He kisses me briefly, then head-points me towards the bathroom. Quickly, I gather up my clothes and my dignity, before vanishing inside.

Assuming that Francis will only be a minute or so, at first I wait, artfully arranging myself to wait for my Master. When he comes in, I want him to find me ready for him.

After five minutes or so, there is no sign of his arriving, so I listen at the door, then peek through. He is in deep conversation with Francis, and the two look as though they will be engaged for some time.

I like Francis, very much. She is the very soul of kindness and courtesy, but *right now...*

Aaarrrgghhh...

Huffing in disappointment, I know that it is my own fault. My Master did, after all, say he needed to work. I'll have to wait.

It is easy for my head to be philosophical, but my still twitching pussy does not agree. Finally, deciding that I need to cool off, I set the shower running and stand underneath, rinsing away passion induced perspiration, and the scent of my own arousal.

It does not help. Water washing over my face, I stand, eyes closed, trying to give myself a little relief, my fingers working at the unfinished task they started. Playing with my red curls, I move further and within, dreaming of my Master about to bury himself in me, my clit responding with sweet fire through my belly.

Working myself harder, hoping that the sound of the running water will cover my own stifled moans, sheer desire courses through me. I want my Master, but he cannot come to me, so I work myself, erotic desperation sending electric pulses through my aching pussy.

My hand is seized and pulled away from me.

"*That* my Lady, is *my* privilege." says my Master's voice.

Startled and abashed, I want to look anywhere but into his face.

"Do you realise, Elizabeth," he continues, "that *this* is where we first met, you and I? Time for a replay of those events, I think."

A cuff snaps around my wrist, and my arm is levered upwards to the shower head, then locked into place.

My other arm follows, and I am bound naked to the showerhead, water still playing over my hair and face, breasts and stomach.

As I finally look at him, my Master is stripped down to his jeans, bare-chested and barefooted. "Francis left five minutes ago. You know,

I was watching your performance there, for some while Elizabeth, and you didn't even notice me. I must have been remiss in my attentions to you."

He shrugs off the jeans. "I could fuck you brainless right where you are, but I think we can take a little longer over it. Do you like the cuffs? They're new. I bought them as a present for you."

The cuffs are bright, shiny and very secure. I could not now release my hands, firmly affixed above me, even if I wanted to. My pulse beginning to race, in anticipation of what is coming, I strain against the cuffs, using their restraint to stretch my belly flat, and raise my breasts, displaying myself to best effect for my Master.

"I have another present for you," he says. And with that, he dangles small, bejewelled clamps in front of me, giving me a good view of them before, one at a time, and slowly, attaching them to my nipples.

The attachment itself does not hurt. Quite the opposite, the mild nip as they gently take hold of my crinkled buds is stimulating. A frisson ripples through me, sending a fresh supply of hot juices running down my thighs, mixing with the still streaming waters of the shower. But my Master does not stop there.

Taking my chin in one hand, he directs my face towards my breasts, making sure that I see what he is going to do. My lips parted in anticipation of what I see is coming, ever so slowly, my Master squeezes on the left nipple clamp.

Pain/pleasure surges through me. Squealing in agony/delight at the pain, my knees give under me and my weight drops onto my shackled wrists. My Master makes no attempt to support me. Instead, my legs splaying as my feet scrabble for purchase on the slippery shower floor, he releases my chin.

With the now free hand, he reaches south, gripping my clit between thumb and forefinger. Simultaneously he both pinches my clit below and squeezes on the other nipple clamp above.

This time, I really scream. the pain sparkles through me, sending waves of arousal pulsating through my swollen cunt. Unable to stand, I hang from my wrists, jerking and heaving as my Master alternately nips at raw nipples and my throbbing bud.

"Oh, God. Oh, *God!* I can't stand it. Please, Master. Please stop."

He does not cease immediately. Instead, he gradually reduces the speed and intensity of his torment, the biting of the clamps lessening bit by bit, until I finally regain control of my legs, and manage to stand up again.

Utterly helpless, panting breathlessly, knowing that my Master can do what he wishes with me, I writhe in sensual expectancy, of what is to come.

Taking down the showerhead, still spraying water, he aims it over my breasts, moving in close, to target my tortured nipples. The sting of the water playing over my skin sends tingles skipping down through me again, further igniting my pussy. Directing the pressure of the water against each of the clamps in turn, making them jingle and jump, my Master sends vibrating fire spinning through me.

Moving slowly down, so that I have a clear idea of where he is heading, the sharp ping of the water over my skin moves down my belly, my loins and thighs, then directly upwards between my legs. My Master is in the shower with me, his erection pressed against my belly, as he forces my feet apart with his, holding my body against the wall so that, arms pinned over my head, I cannot move at all, except to quiver and tremble in anticipation.

The shower head aimed within, the spray moves directly onto my swollen clit.

The sensation is incredible, inescapable. No amount of wriggling or writhing takes my tormented bud away from the exquisite torment of the jet. Each needle of water caresses, nudges and torments my pulsating flesh.

Moving the jet further inwards, the steaming hot water spurts against my pussy. Dropping to his knees, my Master reaches inwards, parts already sensitive lips and directs the water over and in.

The water streams against my inner muscles, swirling and pounding, vibrating and massaging. Playing the water back and forth, he alternates between cunt and clit, directing it over and into my clenching, twitching pussy. I stagger and totter, wailing and howling, with arousal and sheer over-stimulation.

My orgasm builds quickly, rising, sweeping over me in a tsunami, overwhelming me with spasms that pulsate through thighs, belly and cunt. I think I am gushing, but with the heat of the water pounding my core, it is difficult to be sure.

I want to collapse but cuffed to the showerhead cannot. My Master wraps an arm around my waist, raising me and taking some of my weight, relieving the strain on my wrists, but he does not cease his torture of my orgasmic cunt and clit.

Finally, unable to take any more, I scream "Redhead. *Redhead!* Stop, Master. *Please* stop."

Instantly, my Master takes away the water jet, simply supporting me as I sag, limply, into him. Gasping and panting, utterly spent, I lean into his chest, my wet long hair plastered over him.

After long moments, he whispers, close by my face. "And *that* is what happens to girls who tease."

I chuckle but do not have the energy for more. Dripping and sated, I am content simply to rest against my Master, vaguely aware that he has not yet climaxed himself, but not doubting that he will soon wish me to attend to this.

Instead, he says, "I do have another gift for you, Elizabeth. But you must tell me if you are going to accept it."

Puzzled, though intrigued, by this, I say, "I always love your gifts, Master. I'm sure I will accept it."

He is strangely hesitant. "You don't know what it is yet." He uncuffs my left arm, releasing it from the shower head, then reaches for something from a side-shelf. "I was wondering how to offer you this, but when I saw you there in the shower, as you were when we first met that day, it seemed the perfect way to do this."

He opens a small box and offers me the contents.

Stark naked, still tingling with orgasmic after-burn and right arm cuffed above my head to the shower fitting, dripping with water, I look down...

... and gape at what is being offered to me.

A simple gold band, set with a diamond.

A ring.

Speechless, I just stare at it.

After a moment, my Master sounds worried. "Is it too soon, Elizabeth? I'm not upsetting you?" Then he claps a hand to his head. "I'm not doing this right, am I?"

He drops to one knee in front of me, still offering me the ring. "Elizabeth. Will you marry me? Will you be my wife?"

I want to say *Yes.* at the same time, I want to cry; joy and astonishment both welling up in me.

My Master, normally so sure of himself, looks hesitant, upset. Taking my free left hand, he offers the ring to my fourth finger. "May I put this on you, Elizabeth?"

I nod, then finally find my voice again. "Yes, Master... Yes... *Richard.* You may put it on me."

His face lights up, with a smile like the first sunshine after rain, and he slips the ring onto my finger, then stands and embraces me. I would like to embrace him back but settle for a light hug with my free arm.

He finally seems to realise my position and unlocks the remaining cuff. Swinging the limb around a little at first, to get the blood flowing again, I hug him, holding him tightly before he dips his face to mine, kissing me deeply. For minutes, we stand there, together, saying nothing, simply holding each other.

Finally, I ask, "What would you have done if I'd said No?"

He sniffs dismissively. "Cuffed you back up and fucked you 'til you screamed for mercy. Much like the first time we met here, as I recall."

*****

Later:

"Can I ask you something, Master? Richard?"

He gives me a sidelong *look.* I only ever call him 'Richard' when we are in company. In private, between us, he is always 'Master'.

"One of those questions is it? Go on then. But I'm not promising an answer."

"Why didn't you marry Adele? She's so beautiful, and obviously more experienced with life. Why did you ask me and not her?"

He looks away, clearly taking the time to choose his words. "She *is* beautiful, yes, and you're right. In some ways, she is more obviously 'wifely' material for me. But there is something about her that, as I came to know her, it... Well, it repelled me. There's a coldness about her. Beautiful? Yes, she is. But beautiful like a statue. You are so much more *alive* than she. There were other things too."

"Such as?"

"Well, for a start, she was too obviously after the money."

"What makes you think *I'm* not interested in the money?"

He laughs. "You'd be foolish to not be at least a *bit* interested in the money, wouldn't you? And you are anything but foolish. But Adele, when it comes down to it, is not all that bright. She's more worldly than you, less naïve, but not nearly so intelligent. Then too, she tried to make herself dependent on me. You have never done that."

"I'm living with you."

"Yes, but it was at my invitation." He pauses. "Insistence actually, with the danger to you from Mack Kane until we track him down.

Adele tried to simply move in. I arrived one day to find that she'd moved in with her clothes and goods, and taken over one of the rooms. I didn't allow it. She took the huff and left."

He sits beside me, taking my hand in his. "Besides, you are working on your studies. Working hard to make yourself independent. You want to be your own woman, not a just satellite to me."

I shrug. "You don't actually *know* if I'm working hard at it."

He laughs. "Actually, I do. I checked with your tutors."

I glance at him, startled. My Master has been checking up on me?

He continues "I have high confidence that you will do well in your exams. Now and later. You need to do that."

Still holding my hand, but looking down, not meeting my eyes. "The fact is, Elizabeth that, while having you here is something of a dream for me, I am older than you. Quite a bit older. When it comes down to it, I can spend the rest of my life with you, but *you* can't spend the rest of your life with me. When the time comes, I want you to be alright. Not just because you have a pile of money in the bank..."

He chuckles... "... Although I intend that you *do* have a pile of money in the bank. But I want you also, to have the knowledge, the experience and training, in how to handle the money. How to look after the business. How to deal with the people around you. That way, I know that whatever happens to me in later years, you will have a good life."

This talk of my Master being so much older than me is beginning to upset me. We should be celebrating today. My Master suddenly seems to realise that he is sounding gloomy and, almost visibly, shakes himself out of it. Kissing my fingers, he says "Do you like it? The ring I mean?"

The gold gleams warm at me, the diamond bright.

My *ring.*

Given to me by my Master.

"Oh, yes, it's beautiful. How could I not like it? Can I... Can I wear it in public? I mean, do you want people to know?"

He beams at me. "Yes, of *course* I do. I'm proud of you. I want to tell the whole world about us. We'll announce it at the dinner tomorrow evening with the Thorntons. How's that? We'll all celebrate together."

"That would be lovely."

The following morning, since my Master wants to celebrate, to announce our engagement publicly, although I have a wardrobe full of beautiful clothes, I want something new, something really special. How often in a girl's life does she get to announce her engagement?

Time to go *shopping.*

"If you're going," he says, "Take Ross with you."

"Oh, do I have to?" I complain.

Ross has been my shadow ever since Mack Kane attacked me and escaped. Whenever I go out and about, Ross is with me. I like him. He is pleasant company, but I am beginning to long for a bit of space, just some time to myself.

"Mack hasn't been found yet." replies my Master. "It's not safe for you to be out alone."

"I'll be very careful." I promise. "If I see any sign of him, I'll call you immediately."

My Master looks doubtful. I am sure he is going to refuse, so I press my point. "What can he do if I'm in a public place? So long as I can call you, I'm perfectly safe."

"All... right..." My Master is very reluctant. "But I want your promise that you will have your phone on you at all times."

"I promise. At all times. And if there is any sign of Mack, I'll call you immediately."

He jabs a finger towards me. "*Do* that."

Later, Ross drops me off at the department store. "I'll be back in three hours, Beth," he says. "I'll be by the main entrance. Please do be on time, even if it's just to say that you want a bit longer. If I don't keep track of you, he'll have me skinned."

I laugh. "Of course I will." Checking my watch. "Three hours. If anything holds me up, I'll call you."

"You do that." He waggles a finger at me, waves and drives away.

Relieved to have some time to call my own, I wander into the store. I will look for a special dress, then look for shoes, jewelry, and a bag to go with it.

The store has so many beautiful clothes, and I enjoy myself browsing along the aisles, trying on anything that appeals to me. After going through about twenty different outfits, I am hovering between a sparkly blue number that is a bit over-the-top, but so pretty, and a rather more demure and classic, 'little black dress' that would suit any occasion. Deciding to go and have a coffee, while I mull over which I prefer, I hand over the two dresses to the assistant and explain that I will be back in half an hour with my decision.

I turn for the cafe bar, to find myself face to face with Adele. As ever, she is immaculately dressed and perfectly made up, but her beautiful, chiseled features still have that hard edge. Her eyes are cold above her painted-on smile, and I reflect on my Master's comments about her.

"I thought it was you, Elizabeth," she says sweetly, although with an edge to her voice that I don't care for. "I'm so sorry for what happened when we last met. We got off to a bad start, didn't we? I'd love to have a chat with you, get to know you better. Can I buy you a coffee?"

I hardly like to refuse. Adele is being perfectly polite and, well, perhaps we can be friends...

Despite my misgivings, I reply. "That would be nice. I was just going for a coffee myself."

"Such lovely dresses," she comments, looking at the clothes I just passed to the assistant. "But you do have the figure for them, don't you."

As we stroll to the bar, she keeps up a constant chatter, asking me about my Master, *Richard,* my life with him, what we are doing together. At first, I don't want to talk about him; it is rather personal after all, but by the time we are sitting and drinking a couple of cappuccinos, I am beginning to relax. Adele is just trying to be friendly. Perhaps I have been mistaken about her.

"Yes, he's a super person, isn't he," I say. "Such a lovely man."

Adele looks a little startled at this. "*Lovely?* I can't say it's a word I would have chosen. I always found him rather domineering. Arrogant."

"Well, he's a strong man, yes, but he's so kind, so generous," I say. "I mean he's helped me so much with my training for college and everything."

Adele's mood seems to change, her eyes softening. Sitting opposite me, across the table, she stirs her coffee pensively. "I can see why he likes you. You're a sweet kid."

It is so strange. Adele seems suddenly a completely different person to the scheming bitch I have always taken her for, and which everyone else seems to agree she is. Baffled by her altered temper, I sip my coffee, hiding behind the cup as I hold it to my lips.

She gazes absently at me for a moment, just looking, seeming reflective, almost regretful, when her gaze lands on my ring.

She stares at it for a moment, unblinking, before fury washes over her features. Her expression changes completely, her perfect features made ugly by rage. As she flushes red, then white, her complexion turns that odd shade of a woman wearing make-up the wrong shade for her skin colour.

"Is that from *him?*" she hisses. "Did *he* give you that?"

Nervous now at this further abrupt switch of tone, I babble a little. "Well, yes. We're engaged. It's not been made public yet. In fact, we were going to announce it tonight." Beginning to feel afraid, I want to go. Standing, I say "It's been nice to meet you, Adele, to finally have a chat. But I need to be going. I've got things to do."

Quickly I stand to leave, then become aware that Adele is looking at someone over my shoulder. Turning, I find a man, no, two men, standing close to me. Too close.

One has something in a pocket, pointing at me. A knife? A gun?

"Don't argue, Elizabeth," says Adele sweetly. "Just go with these gentlemen where they tell you, and you won't get hurt." She pauses. "Not for now, anyway."

My mouth dry, fear gnawing at me, I turn, looking around, wondering if I dare try to break away. This is a public place. Surely, I can...

"Don't even think about it, Elizabeth," says Adele. "No one else here would see it as it happened and by the time they'd figured it out, it would be far too late for you."

What can I do?

The security cameras? All they can see is a group of people. Nothing to indicate trouble to a security guard, even if anyone is actually monitoring them. And... If Adele is not worrying about her face being seen on camera, she must surely have taken some precaution over cameras?

I am walked through the store, the two men flanking me. One of them holds me tight by the wrist, although to any passer-by, it will simply look as though he has linked arms with me.

The other mutters at me "Just look straight ahead. Don't try to catch anyone's eye. We've just been enjoying a nice afternoon stroll in the shops, and now we're going to the car."

Frightened now, I am wondering where Ross is. How long will it be before he comes looking for me?

What does Adele want? To hurt me? Kill me? Ransom me? Or simple revenge against my Master? Plain jealousy?

They march me out through a side door. A limousine is waiting outside, the windows darkened so that the occupants cannot be seen. One of the men with me opens the rear door, apparently smiling at me, but the smile stops at the mouth. His eyes are hard, like agates. "Do get in, Elizabeth. Make yourself comfortable."

I try to resist, to hesitate, anything to give Ross time to realise that I am late, to raise the alarm. What time is it? It must have been long enough now for him to be looking for me. The man behind me raises what looks to the outside world like a companionable hand to the elbow to guide me in, but I can see his other hand in his pocket, something pointing at me.

Can I drop something? Leave a sign to be found? No, they are watching me too closely. As slowly as I dare, I step into the back of the car, still with a man flanking me on either side. My breathing fast and shallow with fear, I try not to panic, to think clearly. What must I do?

My mobile is in my bag, still with me, but there is no way that I can call from it. Might Ross call me? Probably. Did I leave the ringtone turned on? I can't remember. If the phone rings, it is certain that it will be taken from me.

Biting my bottom lip to control my panic, I clasp my bag closely to my lap, hoping not to draw attention to it.

One of the men fencing me into the seat says "Keep both your hands in view. No clever moves."

Saying nothing, I rest both my hands, palms down, on my bag. Through the soft leather, I can feel a vibration. It is my phone, sound turned off but still with the vibe working. Probably, Ross is trying to contact me. The vibration continues for some seconds then ceases. Then, almost immediately, it starts up again.

Ross is looking for me. That means my Master will very soon also be looking for me. My Master has many friends, in the police, on the streets. He will find me. And he will be so angry with these people; with Adele and these men working for her. I have only seen my Master's rage once before when I upset him. What will he do to these people?

From the front seat, the driver swings around to face me. "Why *hello,* Beth. How nice to see you again." Mack Kane smiles maliciously at me, then turning away, starts the car and drives us away, to be quickly lost in the city traffic.

The Story Continues in 'The Master's Revenge'

Part Ten
The Master's Revenge

As the car drives into the city traffic, I feel the, now almost constant, vibration of my mobile phone through the leather of my bag. Someone, perhaps several someones; Ross, my Master, Francis, is trying hard to contact me. I promised Ross that I would meet him three hours after he dropped me off at the store. The fact that I am not replying to repeated attempts to call me, must be raising the alarm.

The *problem* is that I have been kidnapped. Somehow, Adele, my Master's 'ex' and Mack Kane, the man whose fraud against my Master I inadvertently discovered, have colluded in my abduction, and right now, I am being driven away through the city to destination unknown, by my captors. Both Adele and Mack, I know, wish me ill, but do they simply want me out of the way, or is this an attempt at ransom? An intention to extort money from my Master?

However, whilst having me in their power, they have failed to take my bag. Specifically, it does not seem to have occurred to them that I have my mobile phone and that my friends could be trying to contact me. After a dozen attempts, my Master surely now realises that I am in trouble. If there is an 'up-side' to my situation, it is that my friends are certainly looking for me.

The two men sandwiching me in the back seat of the limousine could be straight out of any 1930's gangster movie; over-built thugs who look as though their knuckles should trail the ground. What did they think I'd be able to do? One slimly built young woman, against these two?

The thug to my left shifts his position a bit, squeezing me further into the already limited space of the rear car seat. At this moment, the phone in my bag chooses to vibrate its call again. Pressed up against me, the thug feels the vibe and turns, startled, looking for the source of the disturbance.

Looking down, he spots my bag and, with a curse, snatches it out of my hands, rummaging through the contents. "There's a phone in here. Someone's trying to call her."

"So, keep it out of her hands." comes a calm voice from the driver's seat. Mack Kane is quite unruffled. "If she can't reply, then it's not a lot of help to them, is it?"

The thug gives me a dirty look and shoves the phone in his own pocket. There is no possibility that I can use it now to call for help. Carefully, I paste an upset expression on my face. It isn't hard. I am already fighting back tears, but this is not the time to break down. And leaning back into the seat, I reflect that it seems my captors are not all that bright and have not thought their way through the implications of modern technology.

I have to play for time. Time is my friend now.

"Where are you taking me?" Neither man either side of me replies. Mack too is silent.

"You won't get away with this you know." I know that I am babbling nonsense, but all I am trying to do is divert their thoughts, to stop them from thinking properly. "Richard has so many friends. In the police, too. They'll be looking for me now."

Mack swings around from the front, the car swerving dangerously as he does so. "Well, they're looking in the wrong place, aren't they? Now shut your trap, before we shut it for you. Unless you want the party to start right now?"

Chilled by the implicit threat in his words, nonetheless, I keep talking. "What are you going to do with me? Ransom me? Is that it? You want back the money you stole in the first place?"

Mack swings around again to look at me. This time the car almost comes off the road. "I told you. Shut it."

He drives to a less appealing part of town; old abandoned warehousing and industrial units. The area is depressing, with very few people apart from a couple of what look like homeless types, curled up in sleeping bags atop, or under, old cardboard boxes. Broken bottles and hypodermic needles are scattered over the ground. No reputable person is going to wander here accidentally. Do they intend to hold me prisoner here? In this awful place?

Mack pulls up at the back of an old warehouse, brick built, run down and empty, several stories tall, but long unused and falling into disrepair. Broken windows access black spaces and pigeon nests. The remains of an old hoist and winch groans in the wind from the top storey.

As I am escorted out of the car, a thug firmly holding me by each arm, Mack says "Don't get any ideas. Konner here..." He indicates the ape to my left. "... has a nasty side and he would love to start celebrations with you early." Again, the tacit threat.

I look at Konner to see the 'gun' still showing through his pocket, aimed right at me. I gaze around, hoping for help from the lost and the lonely curled up in their cardboard shelters. No one even looks at us. We could be invisible for all the notice they take.

I am escorted into the building and up several flights of stinking and graffitied stairs, the pungence of urine hanging over everything, making my eyes sting. Now that we are finally isolated from the rest of the human race, Konner pulls the gun out of his pocket to where I can see it clearly, loosely trained on me. The other of Mack's toughs almost twists my arm out of its socket as he forces me up the steps.

At the top of the stairs, a paint-peeled door swings open to reveal the room's solitary occupant. Adele stares out at me from a chair.

"How lovely to have you here, Elizabeth. And poor Mack is *so* pleased to have you visit us too. You are going to compensate him after all for the trouble you cost him. Put things to rights for him."

"You're ransoming me?"

"Yes, dear. We're going to ransom you. Mack wants his fair payment for all that he was robbed of. I'm sure Richard will be happy to pay for you."

I nod, quite certain of my ground now. "Of course he will pay to get me back."

Mack sneers. "He won't *be* getting you back, though."

Blanking out for a moment. "I thought you said you were going to ransom me?"

"Oh yes, sweetie. We are. But you won't be returning to your precious Richard. Adele here wants you off the scene for her own reasons, and I have other plans for you."

Fighting the fear freezing my guts, I say to Adele "Richard's not interested in you. You had your chance with him, and you blew it."

She rocks her hand back and forth. "Well... *Yes*... Perhaps I did make some mistakes with him. But I know better now. I'll get him back alright, once you're no longer distracting him..."

Again, that unpleasant hint of their plans for me. I do not want to give them the satisfaction of asking, so I remain silent. That way too, I can keep them from hearing the tremble in my voice, the fear gnawing at me.

Mack caves in first. "You're quite the beauty, Beth. All that lovely red hair. Nice pale skin. Quite exotic in some parts of the world you know. I have a couple of buyers lined up for you. I'm not quite sure where they intend to take you. Somewhere in the depths of Asia, I believe. Or was it Africa? I forget, but believe me, once you go with them, you'll not be bothering Adele or me again, and I'm sure you're going to have such fun in your new future."

He grins nastily. "Adele, with the price they're offering for Beth here, how many cocks do you think she's going to have to suck off to pay off the debt to her new owner?"

Adele smirks. "Oh, I wouldn't like to say. Quite a lot obviously. Several dozen a day I should think. And that's if all they want is cock-sucking, which doesn't seem likely of course."

Not trusting my own attempts to speak, I hold my silence, terror pooling in the pit of my stomach. If my Master should not find me in time...

Mack comes up close. *Really* close. I can smell his sour breath. He always made my skin crawl, but now, as his hand slides over my breast, I could vomit. Shrinking from his touch, I try to back away, but he follows, and I have nowhere to go.

"Adele," he says. "Do you want to watch? While we educate Beth here in what will be expected of her in her new life?"

"Wouldn't miss it for the world, Mack," she replies. "Will it just be you or...?"

"Nope," he says. "Konner and Elroy here were promised some of the fun, as part of their payment."

Startled, I look to either side of me where suddenly, the two thugs are flanking me once more. Each takes one of my arms, holding me fixed between them. Mack presses himself against me, sliding a hand under the hem of my skirt, up and in, to my panties. "That's right, Boys. Time for you to relax. It's been a long day. Let's enjoy the fruits of our labours."

His fingers slide inside the crotch of my panties, probing. I try to clamp my thighs together, my breathing growing short and heavy, my heartbeat rising to a panicked crescendo as the reality of what they intend for me sinks in. Fruitlessly I try to resist, but I might as well fight a mountain. The men holding me don't budge, I cannot escape and Mack is pushing his fingers up into my unwilling pussy.

"No!" I yell. "*No!*"

Mack sniggers. "Not your choice now, sweetie. Your choices have been made for you. I'm going to enjoy this."

Adele has settled back into her chair and is pouring herself a glass of wine, with all the air of someone setting up to watch a much-anticipated movie. She might as well be eating popcorn.

As I struggle hopelessly against my captors, Mack says to them, "Just stand back for a minute boys. I can manage her. Don't worry. You can join in the fun soon."

The two release me, standing back. Immediately I try to break away, to run, but Mack snags my ankle with a foot, bringing me crashing to the floor. Grabbing me by an elbow on the way down he crashes a fist into my face.

"Hey!" interrupts Adele. "You can't do that, Mack."

I am momentarily baffled at Adele's intervention, apparently to help me, but she continues "Don't do anything that will leave visible marks. You'll bring her price down with her new owners. Keep her looking pretty."

It feels as though she may be too late for this. Already I feel my eye beginning to swell. Mack's smile is malicious as he looks down at me. "Quite right, Adele. Let's not devalue the goods. We've got plenty of options without leaving visible damage."

Pushing me down to the floor, the palm of his hand on my chest, he says to the two men. "Hold her arms over her head. Give me some room to work."

My arms are snatched at the wrists, tugged up and back. Flat on my back, my arms pinned, Mack kneels between my legs, forcing my knees apart and pushing my skirt up above my waist, leaving me naked below the waist barring my scanty green lace panties. He reaches down to my blouse, ripping it open at the front, buttons *pinging* in all directions as they pop off under stress.

For a moment, he kneels upright, just looking down at me, I think forcing me to wait, to anticipate what is to come, to increase my fear.

"Tell me, boys. Do want to take turns with her? Or shall we all weigh in at once?"

"You first, Boss," says Konner. "Then both of us."

"Then we'll all have her together," says Elroy. "Top and tail her. One down her throat. One over her face. One up her ass."

"There's an idea," says Mack. Still looking down at me, staring me full in the face. "Yeah. I'll have you on your knees. My cock hard down your throat, balls banging your face." And with that, he reaches, grasps the top of my panties and is about to pull when...

... A wailing noise, eerie and strange as it echoes around the room, but to me as welcome as sunshine after rain.

The cavalry has arrived... at *last.*

The sound of police sirens reverberates around us.

Konner dashes to the window, peering down through clouded glass and cobwebs, then says. "There's police cars out there. Lots of them. The building's surrounded."

Fury washes across Mack's face, followed by confusion. Adele's expression is apoplectic.

"How?" she demands. "*How* did they find us?"

They both look at me.

Relief washing over me, still sick to my stomach but nonetheless, relieved, I say, "You figure it out. You're neither of you all that bright, are you?"

Bafflement radiates from both of them...

"Did it occur to you that mobile phones these days do a lot more than make calls? Of course, my friends know where I am. They only had to trace my signal."

They still both look blank. "It's a modern phone," I continue. "A smartphone. They all have GPS built in. And they can all be set to be traceable. Usually it's just a protection against theft, but in this case, it meant that I could be tracked if needed."

Adele's face twists. Mack still looks bewildered. *How* did he succeed in defrauding my Master for so long if he is really this stupid?

From below comes the sound of many feet running up the echoing stairs.

"Put your gun down," I say to Konner.

"Don't," says Mack to him. "We'll fight it out. We'll..."

Konner throws his gun to the ground. Another follows, dropped by Elroy. Mack looks furious. "You're being well paid for this!"

"I was being paid for a job," says Konner. "No one said anything about fighting it out with the police. I'm not being paid for suicide."

The door slams open and my Master bursts in, closely followed by several police officers. To the rear, I see Ross and Francis. Francis' eyes are swollen, as though she has been crying. Ross looks at me, still down on the floor, holding my eyes long, radiating apology.

My Master gazes around the room, taking in the tableau. He looks down at me, his expression bland. "What have they done to you, Elizabeth?" His gaze lingers over my swelling eye, my ripped clothes...

A strange reluctance takes me. I don't want to tell my Master about what has/was going to happen. I am *his.* I don't want to admit that...

... Of *course* I must tell him.

"Not much so far. They didn't have time. It probably looks worse than it is."

I wipe my eye, streaming fluid. Tears? Or blood? "Mack was about to... to... to gang-rape me."

My Master raises an eyebrow, but his expression stays blank, his gaze sweeping over Konner and Elroy. "With these two?"

"With them, yes. They were holding me down when..." My throat seizes up and the words won't come out. Losing my self-control, my tears start flowing, streaming down my face as I try fruitlessly to wipe them away.

Still calm, my Master asks, "And Adele?" He glances at her. Astonishingly, she is still holding her wine glass.

"Adele wanted to watch. And then Mack was planning to ransom me back to you, but sell me anyway to someone in the third world even when you paid. I'm not sure who. A brothel-keeper or people-trafficker I think. That's what he said anyway."

My Master's voice is calm, measured. "Is that right?"

I am not fooled by his calm tones. This is my Master at his most dangerous. He offers out his hand, helping me to stand, his gaze hovering over my ripped clothes, my tear-stained face.

"Francis. Ross. Please take care of Elizabeth. See if she needs medical attention."

Ross removes his chauffeur's jacket, placing it around my shoulders, and then with Francis, takes me by an arm, trying to lead me out of the room, but I resist. I want to see what happens next. Now that my Master is here, in charge, in command, I know that everything will be alright. But I need to know how this ends.

"Adele. Anything to say?" he asks, his stare like the passage of the Angel of Death.

She runs to him. Tries to fling her arms around her. He pushes her away with an expression as though he had just bitten into rotten meat.

"I did it for us," she says. She starts to cry, dabbing her eyes. "I didn't mean her any harm. She's just a kid. But I wanted her to go away so that you and I could be together again."

I have to admit she puts up a good act, but it is all so false. Adele is a snake.

"And for that, you wanted to sit back and watch her be gang-raped? Sold to the highest bidder? While you *drank wine?*"

She falls silent.

"Adele, whatever else happens now. You and I will never be together. It would never have happened anyway, but after what you have done here, and tried to do..." His voice trails away.

He turns his attention to Mack. I cannot help but contrast the two men. My Master, tall, holding himself proud. Mack, slinking, cowering, caught. If Adele is a snake, Mack is a worm.

"And what do you think I should do about you, Mack? You stole from me. Attacked Elizabeth in her own apartment. Now you abduct her, assault her. You were about to rape her and then sell her into sexual slavery? What is the appropriate way of dealing with a man like you?" His voice is calm, but I see the whiteness of his knuckles. My Master's self-control is trigger thin.

He is interrupted. "It's not up to you, *Mr* Haswell," says a voice. "This is a police matter now. I think we'll take it from here. Look after your lady there. That's the best use of your time now."

My Master says nothing, simply gazing toward the Police Chief who has entered the room. He nods and turns away, holding his hand out to me, crooking his fingers in the old 'Come with Me' gesture.

I step towards him, but at that moment, Mack screams and launches himself at me. Taken utterly by surprise - Mack is unhinged - I retreat, but my Master is there, grappling with the madman. The two struggle back and forth, wrestling, fighting. My Master is much the taller and stronger, but Mack is behaving like a lunatic. All the while, he screams dementedly at my Master. He cannot win. He must know this. Even with the small chance that he might overpower my Master, the police are here, guns trained on him. I think they would shoot now, except for the chance of hitting the wrong party.

My Master breaks loose from Mack, throwing, almost hurling, him against the wall. Mack launches himself back at my Master, who sidesteps him. Mack overshoots, directly towards the window, teeters on the edge for a moment, then, screaming, tumbles out.

His scream is caught abruptly short. We all dash to the window to see that, somehow, he has caught hold of the winch and pulley and is dangling from the end, two hundred feet above the hard concrete far below.

My Master hesitates for a moment, then catching the window edge, Ross holding him by the wrist for support, leans far out, reaching a hand to Mack with a *Take It* gesture "Oh, come on, man. You don't seriously have any choice, do you?"

Mack glares at him, cold-eyed. "Fuck you, Haswell." Then, sneering, lets go, and drops.

Shrieking, he falls, lands, then rebounds from an iron paling five floors below, finishing on the concrete of the yard. Even from here, the twisted angle of his neck is obvious. A small crowd from the assembled police vehicles below gathers around the awkward body, but there is no movement from the corpse.

There is silence, no one daring to speak, then Adele's voice drawls, "Well at least that's one less in the courtroom."

Is she really that stupid?

My Master startles as though stung. He strides over to Adele, fury on his handsome face, his hands balled into fists.

Before he can reach her, two police officers block his path and the Police Chief places a placating hand on his chest. "I think *we'll* take it from here, Richard. Don't want you doing anything you regret. Anything that might get you in trouble. We all saw what happened. There's no need to upset yourself over this one. You need to look after Miss Kimberley there."

Screaming hysterically, Adele is led away in cuffs.

"She won't be out of prison anytime soon." says the Police Chief. "By the time they find the key, I should think she'll be quite a different person, certainly a lot older."

My Master flings his arms around me, and I finally feel able to let go, to release the emotions boiling up inside me. Sobbing hysterically, I hide in my Master's embrace as, kissing the top of my head, he rocks me from side to side, I think comforting himself as much as me.

*****

My Master steps over the threshold, carrying me in his arms. My huge white meringue of a dress catches on the handle, and he struggles through the door with me and it together. I giggle, as he makes complex maneuvers trying to get himself, me and the dress all through the door together.

"Welcome home, Mrs Haswell," he says.

Smiling, running his hand over the bodice of my wedding gown, his deep blue eyes are almost glowing. "You look beautiful in this dress, Elizabeth. But on the whole, I think I want to get you out of it."

Sucking my lips in anticipation, "Yes, um, I think you're going to have to help me." The dress is boned, buttoned, laced and cinched in tight.

He looks the dress over from all sides. "Um, yes. I see what you mean. Not so much a dress as a construction. How did you get into it?"

"Francis helped. She did up all the buttons at the back. And the laces."

He starts at the back, tugging at laces, trying to loosen the bodice. After several unsuccessful minutes, during which I become more and more giggly, he begins to lose patience.

"Think I'm going to need oxy-acetylene kit to get through these," he mutters. Then, "Oh, to hell with this! Bend over, woman. Let your husband at you."

"What are you going to do?"

"Find out what you *Something Blue* is."

"You're just an Old Romantic, aren't you.?"

"Wife, I Love You. And in a while, I'm going to *make* love to you. But right *now,* I need to fuck you."

His creamy voice is thick with lust, and my own desire rises to match. This is my *husband.* I love him passionately.

And now we are together.

Forever.

And I want him *inside* me, with a feral passion I would not have credited before I knew him.

Beginning to pant, I bend forward over the back of the couch, as he winches the skirts and hoops of my dress over my head, followed by the train. Enwrapped in layers of silk, satin and lace, blinded in my strange white world, I can see nothing of what he is doing. I cannot smell the hot scent of his arousal, but I hear him quite clearly, an affectionate whisper through the filmy layers of fabric.

"I realise that, traditionally, we should consummate this in the marriage bed, but right now, I have a raging hard-on and a deep need to fuck my wife 'til she bleats." As he rummages through layers and depths of skirts and petticoats, pushing them all up and over me, he finally achieves his destination. I feel the coolth of air, now free to move around my thighs and waist.

"Mmmm... Blue panties," he comments. "Makes a change from green. But the evidence tells me that we don't need them."

He's right. Already, my pussy is warming to the thought of my Master, my husband, 'fucking me 'til I bleat.' I can feel the *evidence*, the growing damp patch on the crotch that invites my Master in.

Fingers tug at the side laces of the flimsy garment, unlacing first one side and then the other. Firm, warm hands run over my now naked derriere, squeezing and cupping, pulling the cheeks apart.

I thrust backwards, hoping to find my Master's shaft, to impale myself on him. Leaning into me, still clothed, he grinds himself against me, his swelling erection bulging through formal dress trousers. As I bite my lip against the tease of pressure against my warming core, longing for more, my Master's fingers wander inwards, parting the lips of my pussy, stroking and teasing. Under my silken tent, shrouded in a cloud of white, I start to moan. He slaps and smacks at my cheeks, sending a silvery thrill running through me and setting my juices running.

"Let's get the blood flowing, shall we? Get you coloured up. A nice red ass. That's what I like."

Pushing two fingers inside, he finger-fucks me briefly. Again, it is a tease, a promise of what is to come. As soon as I lean back into his hand, to take him inside me, he withdraws, fingertips trailing silver fire over my swelling clit as he leaves.

"Wonder what new brides taste like?" His words flutter through me. "Do I shackle you there, or will you behave and spread yourself as a good girl should?" His laugh is low as he speaks, vibrating through my flesh.

I arch my back, raising my hips as far as I can from my prone position. Stretching my legs wide, I open myself as far as I am able, jittery with anticipation, longing for the touch of my lover's tongue, and for his penetration of me.

I feel him, behind me, moving downwardly, and know he is doing it deliberately. He has only to step back and kneel. Instead, he slides slowly down my body, pressing against me as he does so. The rough fabric of his trousers, his belt, the buttons of his formal shirt, all scrape past my pussy and bud as he descends. The knot of his tie... The slight roughened stubble of his chin... The warmth of his lips...

He settles, the heat of his open mouth against my sex, warm breath wafting over my tender, trembling nub, my palpitating core.

His lips press against my folds, sucking them in, mouthing the slick skin. He mumbles a sound of pleasure, wholly sensual, a rumble of lust and longing. I echo the sound, sighing my shuddering pleasure at the lapping tongue, which probes and penetrates my trembling entrance; enfolding my twitching clit.

With long, slow, gradual strokes, starting low with the parting of my lips, within curls, stroking upwards over my swollen nub, through slippery, sensitive skin, into my pussy, then revolving through my inner muscles, swirling through my heated core.

Again, he laps at me. A long, gradual torment of pleasure. I mewl, a small throaty cry of boundless pleasure.

Rinse and repeat.

My Master does not change the rhythm, does not falter. He simply repeats the same pattern, setting an expectation within my flesh of what is to come in the next seconds, until every part of me trembles and shivers, in anticipation of the next moment.

I am afire. Aflame. My burning core, my touch-hungry cunt quivers and quakes, wanting more, demanding fulfilment and I whimper encouragement to my Master.

"You're not cumming like this, Mrs Haswell," he says. "For our first nuptials, I'm going to be inside you when you climax." His tongue withdraws, against my quivering protest, and I feel the rising of his body behind me, before, after a moment of rustling, the sound of clothes being removed, he presses in close.

His sweat-dampened skin rubs against mine, jolting my senses alive within my white shroud. Parting my ankles, widening my stance, he eases gradually into me, stretching me, his shaft nudging my inner self open, before speeding up, his firm body penetrating my softer one, first softly, then harder and more insistently.

Delving into me, his erection, steel clothed in velvet, probes deep within. Sighing as his sheer width stretches me wide, I hear grunts of pleasure, sounds of hunger, deep down, throaty sounds. Despite his obvious need to simply thrust, long and hard, my Master takes the time still to pleasure me, aiming for my sweet spot, grinding and rotating against my inner walls. Already slick, my passage runs hot and wet for him. His jolts turn into my tingles, his thrusts into my pulsations.

His fingers slip around and in front of me, then down, to my already stiff and prominent clit, swishing around in lazy circles. One hand pulling back the hood, the other swipes over the sensitive nub, in a rhythmic flow that leaves me yelping in time to his movements, my Master orchestrating a rhapsody of pleasure through my whole body.

My orgasm is of the kind that consumes from the centre outwards, detonating out through me. As I wail and howl out my climax, my constricting, pulsating cunt becomes the whole world, as violent orgasmic waves wrack my whole body. Shrieking, screaming, I thrash and struggle against the tortured bliss consuming me. Dimly I know that my Master is also climaxing, leaning forward over me, pinning me down by my outstretched wrists as he growls and groans his release. His cock shudders and grinds as it pulses his hot cream into my clenching pussy.

We buck and thrash out our shared release before, blissed out, I sag into dishevelled, panting glory, my Master limp atop me.

After long moments, the layers of silk, gauze and lace encasing me are pulled back and I emerge from my dim white tent, blinking a little in the sudden explosion of light. My Master eases me upright, turns me to face him, lifts me and carries me through to the bedroom, where he deposits me gently on the bed.

As he unknots his tie, stripping off his shirt, he smiles down at me. "Don't worry. I wasn't about to ravish you again *just* yet."

"Of course not, Master. We'll give it five minutes or so, shall we?"

He chuckles as he lies down next to me, his head cradled in the crook of my neck. "Of course, yes. Foolish of me. Five minutes."

His arms lock loosely around me. "I Love You, Elizabeth Haswell."

"And I Love You too, Master."

The Story Continues in 'The Master's Wife'

Part Eleven
The Master's Wife

"So, where are we going?" I am excited. My Master, Richard Haswell, now my husband, has kept me in the dark as to where we will spend our honeymoon.

"You'll see." He sounds, and looks, smug, refusing to say another word on the subject. But, besides smug, he looks wonderful, wearing the plain white linen shirt and black jeans that suit him so well. The white of the shirt sets off his tan and the tightly fitting jeans enhance his... figure.

I am demurely dressed in a white blouse, navy blue, knee-length skirt, and court shoes.

I try a different angle. "How long will we be away?"

My billionaire Master has responsibilities and a heavy work schedule. I wonder if our 'Honeymoon' is destined to be a long weekend only.

The car turns off the main highway. So, we are not going to the airport. Fantasies of sun-kissed beaches and blue seas fade away.

Instead, we follow narrow roads, away from the city entirely, up towards the mountains. After an hour or so, we turn in to a vast gateway, framed with intricate wrought iron rails and stone lions. A long drive curves ahead of us, set within close-clipped lawns. Beech, oak and chestnuts dot the landscape and, way down the hill...

Is that a lake?

"Oh, it's lovely, Richard! Is this the hotel where we're staying?"

His smug-ometer is going off the scale. "It's not a hotel. There's just us."

"Just us?"

"Well, I brought in a few people to cook and clean for us. Ross insisted on being one of them." He tips his head towards our driver, whose grin I can see, even though the back of his head. "But apart from that, yes, just us." He raises an eyebrow. "You *did* want us to be private for our honeymoon, didn't you?"

I start to speak, but the house comes into view.

It is a small mansion, Georgian I think, and graciously designed. Tall windows frame a door set into a deep porch. Half a dozen steps lead up to the entrance. A carriage circle fronts the facade.

It must have cost a *fortune* to hire this place.

"Oh, Richard. It's beautiful. I love it. And yes, of course I wanted us to be 'private.'"

The car pulls up onto the graveled drive. Ross sets about unloading our luggage. My Master steps out, walks around the car and opens my door, proffering his arm. "Would you like to accompany me inside, Mrs Haswell?"

Mrs Haswell. It brings tears to my eyes, the words still too new for the shine to have worn away.

We step into an elegant hall. Beautifully patterned rugs overlay a gorgeous parquet floor. A chandelier above us is paired with a companion that beckons up a long, curved stairway. To my left, I see a sunlit drawing room. To my right is a dining room, laid out for dinner with candelabras and fresh flowers on a long mahogany table.

It is a house from dreams.

Speechless, I simply stand there, staring.

"Don't you like it?" My Master has a worried tinge to his voice.

"How could I not like it, Mas... Richard?" I am conscious of Ross in the background. Whilst we are in public, my husband is *Richard.* In private, he is *Master.* "It's just beautiful."

He leads me upstairs. "I chose a bedroom for us, overlooking the lake," he says. "But we can always change it if you prefer another one."

The bedroom is sumptuous, and the views are to die for. A huge bed takes centre stage in the room. Sunshine slants over red satin covers, scattered with white rose petals. An ice bucket sits on a small side-table, chilling a bottle.

"Ah champagne!" says my Master. "Let's start with a toast, shall we." He pops the cork and pours two glasses.

We toast. "To us."

"To us."

I sip mine, sniffing at the bubbles up my nose. "I feel as if I'm in a fairy-tale, Master."

He puts his glass carefully to one side and stands before me, hands resting on my waist, face tilted down to mine. "I wanted us to have a beautiful honeymoon. And I want us to have a beautiful life. You deserve a fairy-tale."

Then he grins wickedly. "But there's more."

"Really?" I am excited now, like a kid working my way through a candy jar. Each sweetie seems better than the last. "What? What is it?"

"You'll see. Now, do you want to unpack? Have a bath? Take a walk?" He is being polite, but there is a speculative look in his eye which sets my pussy purring.

"Um... this is our honeymoon. I thought we might find some other things to do? And besides, I want to show you *your* wedding present."

"*My* wedding present?" That eyebrow lifts again and his mouth twitches as his blue, *blue* eyes scan me over. "What *are* you wearing under there?"

I must be completely predictable. He's not been fooled for a minute. "Why don't you find out..."

He looks me up and down, a glint of humour crinkling his eyes, then, standing back, arms akimbo, he nods down at my blouse. "Take it off."

It is an *instruction*. And I always obey my Master's instructions.

Slowly, I start to unbutton the blouse, allowing the slinky fabric to slip to one side, revealing what I am wearing beneath. As the blouse opens, displaying black leather and lace, chrome fittings and buckles, my Master's head tilts to one side, eyes widening and I see the fit of his jeans grow tighter.

"All the way off." His voice is thick.

There is a knock at the door and Ross' voice. "Mr Haswell. Mrs Haswell. I've got your suitcases. Should I bring them in?"

"Later, Ross," barks my Master. "Go and get some lunch."

There is a thump outside - as of suitcases being dropped onto a thick carpet, and the sounds of footsteps retreating down a staircase. A moment later, the sound of a door opening then closing, and the hum of a car engine. Gravel crunches under wheels, then fades.

"No more interruptions." My Master turns the key in the door lock and then turns to me. "You've brought plenty of clothes? Your cases seemed heavy enough."

I'm puzzled. "Yes of course."

"Good." He seizes my blouse inside both shoulders and rips it off me. Seams rip under his un-gentle treatment and my pulse races.

Then he seizes my skirt by the waistband, tearing it in two. It shreds at the fastenings, dropping to the floor. My pussy convulses, gushing. I stand, clad in a black leather corset, stockings and tiny black lacy panties.

"They can go too." My Master slips fingers inside the panties, sliding over my wet clit, testing me, then pulls, and the tattered remains of my panties drop to the floor. "You'll not be needing those for some time... Now then, Mrs Haswell. Let's see about your marital duties. Stand up straight. Turn around. I want to admire my new wife."

Obediently, I turn. He passes me my champagne flute. "Enjoy your wine."

Sipping carefully at my drink, I pose for my Master. His eyes linger on my breasts, cupped high and curved in their leather confinement. He strokes them, slowly, caressingly, and then, peeling down the leather support, eases each one out of its cup so that it sits, pert and displayed, above the corset.

In the cool air, my nipples stiffen and crinkle. For a moment, my Master bends to suckle at one, then, dipping his fingers in my champagne, paints chilled wine over each nipple. The pink buds respond, hardening to nubs, which my Master pinches, enough to make me yelp.

"No noise," he says. "You have to be quiet." Then he pinches again, harder.

This time, I stifle the yelp, but my melting pussy trickles down inside my thighs.

"If you can't be quiet," he says. "I may have to punish you. So be good." And he bends again, to nuzzle at my breasts, biting gently.

I want to bring this to a head. I want to be fucked. My quivering pussy demands it. I decide to speed things up a bit.

Turning the glass in my hand upside-down, I pour icy champagne down the length of my Master's back.

Now *he* yelps, standing suddenly, bolt upright. I collapse into a fit of giggles, making no resistance as my Master grabs me and spins me, bending me over the back of a chair, pulling my ass up and out. Looking backwards through a waterfall of my own long red hair, I catch a glimpse of his expression: laughing/stern. He tries to maintain his poise and authority but is having difficulty.

His hand sweeps down on my *derriere,* slapping hard against one cheek, making me gasp and jump. But my pussy flutters a welcome.

"That, Elizabeth," he says "Was *very* naughty. I am going to have to change my plans on what I had in mind for you today."

"I'm sorry, Master." I splutter to stop myself from laughing. "It seemed like a good idea at the time."

Slap! The hand comes down on the other cheek, stinging. "I'm not going to stop this now," he continues, "until your rear end matches your hair."

Since my hair is brilliantly red, my butt is in for some hard attention. At the thought, my clit begins to pulse. How far will my Master take this?

Slap! This time, the slap is followed by my Master repositioning me, forcing my ankles further apart with his shoe, bending me further forward and pulling open my butt cheeks to fully expose my pink and swelling pussy and clit.

Dropping to his knees behind me, my Master stretches me open with his fingers, licking out the inside of my pussy, sucking up my flowing juices. I moan ecstatically as my inner muscle quiver and jump.

Then he stands and slaps again, first one, already glowing, cheek, then the other.

Twice more, he spanks, moving his hand to different areas of skin. Then he drops again, this time lapping his tongue over my twitching bud. He whirls his tongue in circles, winding the swollen nub in spirals that, with each circuit, send electricity sparking through my core.

Then again, he stands and *slaps.*

He develops a kind of rhythm, standing and kneeling, spanking and sucking, slapping and licking. Again, and again he repeats this. My abused ass is glowing, my honeyed clit rhapsodic.

I am incandescent, afire, wailing my mounting arousal as my Master works his magic on me.

Abruptly, he breaks his rhythm.

Standing again, instead of spanking me, he unzips, pulling out his long, thick cock, and plunges deep inside my slick passage, ramming home. His arms encircling me, he reaches for my clit and, over my screeches, starts tweaking and kneading, flicking and rotating, all the while pumping me from behind.

It is an irresistible combination. Orgasm bubbles up inside me, winging its way through clit and cunt and heart. With a yell of triumph, I squirm and writhe in my Master's firm grasp as he continues slamming my molten cunt. Seconds later, I feel and hear his climax also. He drives home into me, balls bouncing against me and hips grinding as he shudders me full of his hot cum.

With a grunt, he pulls out, standing up straight, and slaps me on the ass one last time. "Not bad for a first shot, would you say, Elizabeth? The first of many I think, over the next few days."

*****

Seating myself in the dining room, appetising smells drift past. "Something smells good," I comment to the figure standing next to me, then start in surprise. It is Ross, resplendent in a fully-fledged butler's uniform and holding a silver tray with soup tureen. He looks rather smart.

"Ross? I didn't know you were a butler too. I thought you were just Richard's driver."

He winks sideways at me. "Don't know all my secrets yet do you, Mrs Haswell?" Then he leans in close to me for a moment, speaking quietly. "About earlier, Beth. Sorry if I caught you at an awkward moment. But I can take a hint as well as the next man."

I try to look demure, sophisticated, but know that I am failing. Ross and I have been solid friends for some while, and he knows me rather well. "That's quite alright, Ross. But it is our honeymoon after all."

Richard glances over from the other side of the table. I don't believe he can have heard what was said, but I think he gathers the gist well enough. He smiles, a glint of humor in his eyes, and turns his attention to removing the cork from a bottle of red.

"That's my job, Mr Haswell," protests Ross.

"I can handle a good bottle of wine as well as you can. You serve the meal and then take the rest of the evening off. I think you'll find there are some very good pubs in the local village."

Ross stays silent, but nods his head in acknowledgement, clearly *taking the hint* for a second time.

The meal is wonderful. Beautifully cooked and skillfully presented, the portions are just enough to feel satisfied, without being bloated. Although the dining table is huge - it would easily seat twenty - my Master and I sit together at one end, candlelit and warmed by a glowing log fire. Contently cradling my wineglass, not feeling the need to speak, I am happy simply to sit, watching my wonderful new husband.

"Thank you for my 'wedding present,'" he smiles. "I'll enjoy it further as we make use of it again later." He winks at me, and a familiar warm rush seeps through my thighs.

"And in fact," he continues, "I have a wedding present for you too."

"Oooh... What is it?"

My Master pushes an envelope toward me. I take it and look at it a bit blankly. I'd been expecting jewellery perhaps, or perfume.

"Well, *open* it," he says, exasperation in his voice.

Inside is a document. I read the top few lines. *Register of Title: Elizabeth Haswell née Kimberley...*

I read on. It is the ownership document for some property or other. I don't understand what I'm looking at.

Perplexed, I look to my Master. "What is it?"

"Those are the title deeds for this house."

My jaw actually drops. The house must be worth... *millions.* Speechless, I just stare at him.

He continues, "As I have said to you before, Elizabeth, I am older than you. Quite a lot older. I want you to be secure. It was difficult before, to gift you property. There are all sorts of complications with tax and so forth. But now that we are married..." He shrugs and smiles... "... those problems vanish."

His forehead creases. "You do *like* the house, don't you?"

Spluttering out my words, "Well yes, of course I do. It's an amazing house. But I thought... well... I just assumed... that you had rented it for a couple of weeks, for our honeymoon."

He shrugs again, spreading his hands in a *don't-blame-me-for-your-assumptions* look. "Now you know..."

There is chuckling from the far end of the room. It is Ross, trying, and failing, to keep a straight face. His formal *buttling* behavior is gone. Instead, he is almost doubled over, pointing at me and laughing. "Oh, Beth. The *look* on your face..."

Clearly, Ross was in on the joke.

"Richard. I don't know what to say. Thank you is inadequate."

"And un-needed," replies my Master. "Thank *you,* for marrying me."

He shoots a look back over his shoulder at Ross, head-pointing him to the door.

"I'll be off then, shall I?" he says. "Goodnight, Mr Haswell. Mrs Haswell. Have a pleasant evening. I'll see you in the morning when you're ready for breakfast."

Ross leaves, leaving my Master and me alone together.

"There's more to the house, Elizabeth. You've not seen it all yet."

Mentally I trace my route through the house; upstairs, downstairs, out through the gardens...

What have I missed?

"Really? Where?"

"I didn't want to show you until everyone had left for the night. Come with me... Um..." He looks me up and down speculatively. "Are you still wearing my 'wedding present'?"

Oh, yes.

Definitely.

Who knows when my Master might be wanting 'marital benefits' again?

"Yes, Master. I am."

"Good. Follow me."

He leads me through the long hallway, to the back of the house, past the kitchens, and to the rear staircase.

Once of a day, this staircase would have been for the use of servants only, so that their lords and masters did not have to pass them on the main, and much more glamorous, front staircase. Dark and dingy, it leads up to storerooms, utility areas and the rear servants' access to the upper hallway. Also, I now realise, it must lead down too.

An oak door blocks the way, the timber ancient, and looking capable of holding off the Hordes of Genghis Khan.

My Master winks at me with an air of mystery, then produces a large skeleton key. "This is our *private* area." The lock sticks, then grinds open. "I must get some oil on this," he mutters.

The door swings back, and cool damp air wafts out. Cellars?

Of course, cellars. A house like this would have had butteries, cold storage rooms, the butler's pantry, laundry areas. And they would all occupy the basement areas, where the gentry would never go.

We descend a flight of uneven stone steps, dimly lit by a single bulb, to a long, arched hallway. Stone flagged and chilly, also badly lit, it leads perhaps fifty yards before ending in what looks like a small chapel. Looking up, the barrel-vaulted ceilings are quite beautiful. Several large wooden doors lead off the corridor to right and left. A glimmer of what my Master intends begins to dawn on me.

His mouth twitching at the corners, he waves me forward. "Want to explore?"

Do I!

Yes, indeedy!

The first door to my left creaks open and specks of rust fall off corroded hinges. It seems to be an old laundry. Stone troughs, with hand pumps, sit side by side with an enormous washing machine straight out of the 1950s. A smell of oil suggests there is a boiler room somewhere beyond. I pull the door closed and move on to the next room.

This is the boiler room. A maze of pipes, valves and complicated machinery weaves through cobwebs draped with the dust of years. A couple of drying racks for washing hang from the arched roof, their ropes filthy, pulleys rusted with age.

My Master, behind me, comments, "All of this downstairs area needs refurbishing. We'll get in the builders and decorators when you've decided what you would like to do with them."

Do with them?

I hadn't got that far. I'm still goggling over the immensity of what my Master has given me. But it occurs to me that these dilapidated rooms, for all their dust and cobwebs, would make wonderfully atmospheric dining rooms for dinner parties. I move on to the next room.

I detect a change in my Master.

Expectation?

What is he up to?

As I push open the door, instead of the chill damp, which has greeted me from the previous chambers, warm air washes over me. The room is warm and glowingly lit, with dozens of fat candles, their light reflecting from polished brass sconces and holders. A fire burns in a huge hearth at the far end of the room, its flames casting shadows, that dance and play over stone walls cleaned and polished to a gleaming finish. Thick rugs scattered over the stone flag floor absorb the chill thrown up from the ground.

I glance back. My Master's eyes gleam. Then I step into the room, taking in more of the detail.

The chamber has been, I think, a dairy, or perhaps a meat store. Long stone slabs of shelves, some with boxes and containers, line one wall. Huge metal rings embedded in the vaulting suggest that whole carcasses might have once hung there, ready to butcher. Then I see the huge, embedded meat hooks alongside them, confirming my thoughts. Now, knowing my Master's... *inclinations...* I know there is another use for them.

Centered in the chamber, there is a colossal bed, a four-poster. Only just fitting under the highest point of the arched stone ceilings, it must have been brought into the room in pieces. It looks old. Solid timber posts, perhaps oak, dark with age, spiral up from the floor to crossbars which support heavy velvet curtains, currently pulled open from the bed itself. Silk cords, attached to the posts at one end, drape across the bedspread.

Before I am able to fully explore this wonderful room, my Master is behind me, holding me close by the waist, controlling me.

"Now, Madam. About my wedding present..." From behind his fingers slide into the front of my blouse, and pull, hard. Buttons fly in all directions and the delicate silk fabric rips apart as he pulls the remains of the garment down from my shoulders and off. My skirt is harder for him, but my Master is a strong man. Seizing the waistband, he tears it apart and the shredded garment drops as my Master methodically strips me.

I wonder how much of my wardrobe will remain by the end of our honeymoon. When I have protested his treatment of my clothes in the past, my Master has simply commented that it is one of the privileges of wealth. What do I think he works so hard *for?* And then he has increased my allowance to buy replacements.

Stripped to my leather corset and stockings, he marches me to the middle of the room, centred between two of the ceiling rings. "Arms up," he instructs, not smiling now, but intense, concentrated.

I raise my arms. "Stay like that," he orders, before going to one of the stone shelves and taking something from a box.

He brings shackles, heavy, solidly made, chains with metal cuffs. Holding my eyes as he does so, my Master clips one end to a ceiling ring. The other is snapped onto my left wrist. The cuff is padded with a soft suede and it won't dig in, but never would I escape these. The snug way they fit my wrists suggests that they are custom made for me. My Master clicks the cuff closed, then shackles my other wrist.

Stretched skywards, I am not uncomfortable, and can stand easily enough. But he shoves my ankles apart, spreading me and knocking me off-balance. I stagger. Were it not for the support from my restraints, I would fall. Revisiting the box, he returns with a spreader bar. Dropping to his knees, he fits it to my ankles, and then winches it a little further open, spreading my legs more widely apart.

Still kneeling, his face level with my moistening crotch, he pulls the satin of my panties to one side. He scents my red curls, my warming sex, then splays my lips with delicate fingers, probing with his tongue for my clit. Teasing it from hiding, he licks it softly, manipulating it. My heated thighs and groin a-trembling, I start to pant and groan. Then again, he rips, and the panties drop to the floor.

My Master ceases his gentle torment. Standing again, he whispers close to me "Not too much yet. You have to be good first."

Now supported from my wrists, my stomach muscles taut with tension, my arms straining as they semi-support my weight, I stand displayed.

My Master circles me, wearing an almost predatory expression. His fingers curl through my long red hair, caress my shoulders and waist, stroke my breasts before he stands back, surveying me, devilment in his eyes.

"Feeling horny, Elizabeth?" he asks, before dipping his fingers between my thighs, running them through folds warm and wet with arousal, probing my swelling pussy. "Ah yes. I thought so." He sucks his fingers clean. "As wet as it comes, and horny as hell."

He returns to the box on the shelf, this time producing one of his favorite toys; a flogger that I once gave him as a birthday gift. Red and black leather, soft and supple, it snaps across his fingers as he tests it, experimentally, on his own hand.

He trails the pliant lashes over the tops of my breasts, their lower halves encased in the leather cups of the corset.

"Hmmm," he muses. "That won't do. That won't do at all." And slowly, locking eyes with me as he does so, he unlaces the top few strands of the bodice, releasing my breasts.

My breasts are large, and normally a little pendulous but, straining upwards as I am, they are raised high on my ribcage, nipples puckering hard with arousal. My Master trails the tails of the flogger over the stiffening nubs, sending tingles down through my stomach to my fluid pussy. He smiles in satisfaction as I moan and tremble, teasing at my nipples, flicking them gently with the leather tresses. I quiver, helpless in my constraints.

I know my Master will fuck me soon, but he likes me to be ready for him. He wants me dripping, begging for his cock inside me. Until then, he will play his games, make me wait.

Unbuttoning his shirt, he strips it off, revealing his well-muscled body. Broad-shouldered and tight waisted, skin gleaming gold in the candle-light, he is such a handsome man; my wonderful Master. Almost from the moment we first met, I wanted him. I want him *now,* inside me.

He steps back and for the first time, really swings the flogger. His aim is perfect. With a snap, the lashes sting past the very tips of my right nipple, biting in as they hum past. I scream and my engorged cunt gushes, hot juices trickling down between my legs. The pain is fleeting; barely there before it is gone again, but my Master repeats the move on my other breast and, as I cry out, I writhe in my bonds, trying to escape *(embrace)* this pain *(pleasure).*

Stalking around me, he lashes, the tails of the flogger licking across my buttocks and the back of my thighs. Each stroke is a little harder than the last, the bite a little deeper, the pain a little more intense. I know that my Master will continue to build the pain until I shout my safe word.

He continues to lash. Before me again, the flail swipes squarely across my breasts, drawing red weals across my Celtic-white skin.

"Not enough yet, Elizabeth? You know you have to ask."

He lashes again, aiming this time at the tender skin inside my thighs. "Until you ask me, I won't stop to let you suck my cock." Through a haze of ecstatic arousal, I see the size of the bulge in the front of his jeans. When he finally fucks me, I'm going to have my brains pinned to the wall.

Another lash. This time, the leather tips kiss up between my legs, biting at my pulsing clitoris. I scream and my knees give, dropping my full weight onto my wrists.

My Master seizes me by the waist, propping me up on my hobbled feet again. "Enough, Elizabeth?"

The words trickle from me. "Yes, Master." My safe word. "*Redhead,* Master."

He still supports me, one strong arm taking my weight. "So, what now, Elizabeth?"

I have trouble speaking. "I want to..." I correct myself. "*May I* suck you off, Master?"

"You may. But because you allowed this to continue longer than it should, I am not going to completely release you."

Still supporting me, he reaches up, unclipping first one wrist, then the other. However, he does not release me. Chaining my two wrists together, leaving the ankle bar in place, he lowers me to my knees. I sag down, exhausted and trembling with over-arousal.

"Kneel up," he orders.

I struggle to obey, hampered by my fettered, widely spread ankles, supporting my shackled hands against him. When I am upright to his satisfaction, he unbuckles his wide leather belt and steps out of his jeans. His cock, released, is hard and tall. Standing proudly towards his taut abs, it quivers to his heartbeat. I know that I will have difficulty accommodating it in my mouth, but I welcome it. He seizes me by the back of the head, gripping my hair, twisting it enough for discomfort. Pulling my face towards him, my Master guides his cock to my mouth, and I part my lips to take it.

"Wider," he orders, pushing between my lips.

I try, struggling to take the thick shaft. I cannot truly suck off my Master like this, shackled and bound. I am simply a receptacle for him. His briny-sweet pre-cum trickles across my tongue but gagged by his bulging cockhead, I cannot swallow, and it dribbles down from the corner of my mouth.

He thrusts, but gently, sliding in and out between my lips, each thrust a little deeper towards my throat. The scent of his musk is delectable. The pulse-beat throb of my Master's wonderful cock vibrates through my mouth. The silky soft skin of the head slips through and over my lips and tongue, pressing in.

My Master, still gripping me by the hair says softly "Do you want me to fuck you, Elizabeth?"

I cannot even nod. I cannot speak, but I try. A gurgled splutter escapes my cock-plugged throat.

"I think that was a Yes?' He withdraws from my mouth, leaving me slavering, and with an aching jaw. "*Was* that a Yes?"

"Yes, Master."

"Yes, what?"

"Yes, Master. Please will you fuck me."

He smiles down at me, soft-eyed. I feel cherished. "That's better. How do you want me to fuck you? Gently or hard?"

"Hard Master. I like you to fuck me hard. But please, can you cum in my mouth at the end. I want to taste you."

He releases his grip on my hair, stroking my head for a few moments. "Good girl. I'll unshackle you now. Then get onto the bed. Lie on your back."

He releases me from the cuffs at wrist and ankle, and I crawl, stiff-muscled towards the bed. My Master sees my difficulties, and scooping me up in his arms, dumps me on the covers.

"Madam. You have let things go too far."

Perhaps he is right. As I lie back on soft, warm blankets, the weals on my buttocks sting. But I don't care. The pain sets me afire. Tomorrow I may pay for this, but right now, I want my Master inside me. I arch my back, raising my hips, offering him my volcanically aroused cunt.

He looks down at me. "I don't think so," he says. And instead of mounting me, he kneels between my legs, swinging them over his shoulders, and presses his mouth to my sex.

I am molten. My gaping pussy welcomes him as he sucks at my lips, lapping at me, swirling his tongue through my entrance. But only briefly.

Slipping two fingers inside me, he gently works my G-spot, whilst his tongue and lips ravish my pulsating clit.

I shudder and squeal as my Master's tongue works me, probing and manipulating my bud in a tick-tock cadence that brooks no resistance. The slight scrape of his stubble on my swollen flesh only heightens the sensations, as I start the swift ascent to orgasm.

Already brinking, my Master's rhythmic attentions to my clit tip me over the edge to release. The heat of his mouth, consuming me, swells and blooms, shattering through my core, and crashing on outwards.

My pulse racing, I feel the pounding of my heart under my ribs, hear my own howl of exultation.

It becomes too much. Too *much*.

"Master. Stop!" I yell. "Redhead! Please. *Redhead*."

He pulls away immediately, climbing over me to straddle my chest. Pushing a pillow under my head, he shoves his cock at my mouth. "Go on then," he says, his voice husky. "This is what you wanted."

This time my hands are free. I can move, at least a little, under my Master. Taking his cockhead in my mouth, I work the shaft with one hand, massaging his crinkling balls with the other.

He is already close. I can feel it at the base of his cock. I knead the root, hard, pressing my fingers in, working up the tension I feel building there. Whirling my tongue around the ridge of his shaft, I suck at the steady stream of pre-cum, using it to lubricate my lips as I squeeze and mouth at the head.

He grunts, a deep, guttural sound that vibrates down through his chest and thighs, and through me.

The pulsing throbs through my fingers as I work his root, and my mouth floods with his hot cream. It pumps and pulses over my tongue, and eagerly I swallow. Looking up at my Master, his head is flung back, eyes squeezed shut, as he pumps his climax into me.

After long moments, he gasps and shudders a frisson down the length of his body. "Oh God! That was good!"

Then, after a moment, "Elizabeth. Could you please relax your death-hold on me now? Should we ever decide to have children, I'll be needing those parts of me in working order."

I splutter and laugh, and he whips himself away. Then he lies down, warm beside me, encircling me with an arm.

He strokes my face. "I love you, Elizabeth Haswell. And you're so sweet. How did you fall for me? I know it wasn't the money."

"I can't pretend that the money's not nice, Master. But I think I would have fallen in love with you anyway. And you with me."

He nestles his head into the crook of my neck. "Yes, I'm sure of it." Then he jerks his head up again. "And what do you think of your wedding present? Now that you've, um, *sampled* more of it."

"Oh, it's fantastic, Master. What else can I say? I might even invite you back into my dungeon from time to time."

He snorts and snuggles up again. "Try to fuckin' well keep me out... Just try..."

"Yes, Master."

Want to Read More about Richard and Beth?

See the new series

The Billionaire's Bride

simone-leigh.com/series/billionaires-bride/

About the Author

Award-Winning author Simone Leigh is English, but lives in Spain with *Him* and her rag-tag collection of rescue dogs and cats.

Here, she divides her time between renovating her beautiful *Casa Rurale* (heavy emphasis on the *Rurale*), swimming naked in her pool and writing red-hot romance and thrillers.

Her steamy thriller series, 'The Master's Child', was the winner of the 2019 'Page Reaper' Readers' Choice Awards in the BDSM & Ménage Categories. Part One of the series, 'Target', was winner of the Reader-Voted #BestBook from the 'Inks and Scratches' Summer Splash Book Awards.

Simone is assured by one internet troll that she is 'Beyond Redemption'.

Also By Simone Leigh

Mastering the Virgin

Part 1 - Friends
Part 2 – Partners
Part 3 – Allies
Part 4 – Comrades
Part 5 – Rivals
Part 6 – Lovers
Part 7 – Masters
Part 8 – Dominants
Part 9 – Suitors
Part 10 – Penitents
Part 11 – Confidants
Part 12 - Champions
Part 13 – Triad
Part 14 – Alphas
Part 15 – Guardians
Part 16 – Hunters
Part 17 – Saviours
Part 18 – Family

***

Charlotte's Search

Part One – Her Master's Wedding
Part Two – Her Lovers' Touch
Part Three – The Sin of the Parent
Part Four – The Daughter's Manumission
Part Five – The Father's Betrayal
Part Six – The Shadow of Obsession
Part Seven - The Loss of Innocence
Part Eight – Her Mother's Love
Part Nine – Her Enemy's Promise

***

Buying the Virgin

Book 1 - The Virgin - Auctioned
Book 2 - The Virgin - Sold
Book 3 - The Virgin - No More
Book 4 - The Virgin – Unleashed
Book 5 – The Virgin – Fulfilled
Book 6 – The Virgin's Holiday
Book 7 – The Virgin's Christmas
Book 8 – The Virgin's Valentines
Book 9 - The Virgin's Master
Book 10 - The Virgin's Lover
Book 11 – The Virgin's Fantasies
Book 12 – The Virgin's Choices
Book 13 – The Virgin's Summer – Part One
Book 14 – The Virgin's Summer – Part Two
Book 15 - The Virgin's Summer – Part Three
Book 16 - The Virgin's Summer – Part Four
Book 17 – The Virgin and the Masters – Part One
Book 18 – The Virgin and the Masters – Part Two

Book 19– The Virgin and the Masters – Part Three
Book 20 – The Virgin and the Masters – Part Four
Book 21 – The Virgin and the Masters – Part Five
Book 22 – The Virgin and the Masters – Part Six
Book 23 – The Virgin's Wedding
Book 24 – The Virgin's Real Christmas

***

The Master's Child

Part 1 – Target
Part 2 – Ransom
Part 3 – Hostage
Part 4 – Kirstie's Christmas
Part 5 – Predator
Part 6 – Prey
Part 7 – Fatale
Part 8 - Vitale
Part 9 – Natale

***

The Lover's Children

Part 1 – Winter Wedding
Part 2 - The Idylls of March
Part 3 – April's Tears
Part 4 – Solstice
Part 5 – Summer's Inferno
Part 6 – Autumn's Fury

***

Bought by the Billionaire

Prequel - Beth
Book 1 - The Master's Maid
Book 2 - The Master's Contract
Book 3 - The Master's Courtesan
Book 4 - The Master's Desires
Book 5 - The Master's Fantasies
Book 6 - The Master's Obsession
Stand-Alone Story – The Master's Birthday
Book 7 - The Master's Sin
Book 8 – The Master's Heart
Book 9 The Master's Rage
Book 10 – The Master's Revenge
Book 11 - The Master's Wife

***

The Billionaire's Bride

Part 1 – The Master's Honeymoon
Part 2 - The Master's Gift
Book 3 - The Master's Love

***

Kirstie's Tale

Part 1 - A Dream of White Horses
Part 2 – An Illusion of Happiness
Part 3 – The Gathering of Storm Clouds
Part 4 – A Conspiracy of Ravens

***

Submissive to Her Master

Book 1 - Enslaved

Book 2 – Enthralled

Book 3 – Entranced

Book 4 – Enticed

***

Call of the Wild

Book 1 - Freedom

Book 2 - Thralldom

Book 3 - Retribution

Book 4 – Revelation

Book 5 – Redemption

***

Tales of Blood and Darkness

Red as Blood

White as Bone

***

Standalone

Hearts of Fire. Poems of Love, Romance and Erotica
Shieldmaiden
Trio – Three Short Stories

***

More details of any of Simone's titles,
plus all her latest stories, at
simone-leigh.com/books

Useful Links

Suggested Reading Order for Charlotte's Story

simone-leigh.com/suggested-reading-order-for-buying-the-virgin

***

Timeline Infographic

simone-leigh.com/timeline-infographic-for-buying-the-virgin

Follow Simone

Website

simone-leigh.com

Bookbub

bookbub.com/profile/simone-leigh

GoodReads goodreads.com/author/show/15454039.Simone_Leigh

Facebook Group

facebook.com/groups/simonessecretrosegarden

Facebook Page

facebook.com/perfumepetalsandthorns

YouTube

youtube.com/c/SimoneLeigh-Author

Instagram

instagram.com/simoneleighauthor

Newsletter Sign-Up

simone-leigh.com/my-newsletter

Contact Simone

simone@coffeebreakerotica.com

www.ingramcontent.com/pod-product-compliance
Ingram Content Group UK Ltd.
Pitfield, Milton Keynes, MK11 3LW, UK
UKHW041827200726
13854UKWH00002BA/612

9 798215 847831